A TREASURED LILY

A TREASURED LILY

A MARSDEN ROMANCE BOOK TWO

DAWN BROWER

This is a work of fiction. Names, characters, places, and incidents are products of the author's imagination or are used fictitiously and are not to be construed as real. Any resemblance to actual locales, organizations, or persons, living or dead, is entirely coincidental.

A Treasured Lily Copyright © 2015 Dawn Brower

Cover art by Victoria Miller

"He's more myself than I am. Whatever our souls are made of, his and mine are the same."

— EMILY BRONTË

CONTENTS

A wise person told me that if I decided to write I needed to create a world that crossed over numerous books. I never set out to write and when I wrote my first book I never imagined the possibility of writing another book featuring those characters. My son is the reason I am continuing on and imagining ways to keep these characters alive. So this book and many more are because of him. Nathan thanks for inspiring me to write more, even if you are too young for me to allow you to read these books right now. Someday maybe you will. I love you.

I also want to acknowledge the usual suspects, my awesome beta readers: Christina S, Cheryl R, Capri B, and Amanda S. You gals rock!

CHAPTER ONE

"I just don't think it's a good idea."

"Nonsense." Lilliana Marsden looked up at her best friend, Lady Gemma Kemsley, and frowned. "It's a brilliant idea. My father is being unreasonable about allowing me to travel to America. The plantation in South Carolina is my inheritance. It's about time I claimed it."

"It's not going to work for you to just show up and claim it though. I don't get why you are in such a hurry. You know full well you won't inherit it until you marry." Gemma reached up and smoothed over her sanguine curls, tucking a loose strand behind her ear.

"Well, that's not entirely true." Lilliana's lips twitched into a cheeky smile; it helped to have a little insight into how her parents worked. Gemma didn't know how much she'd gotten away with over the years. Eavesdropping had become a habit of hers. A person could find out the most interesting things quite by accident. When she overheard her parent's most recent conversation she couldn't help the glee that filled her soul. Reining in her excitement had taken an enormous amount of restraint. She needed to leave England and start the life she envisioned for herself. One she had complete control over. Her parent's still hoped she would settle down and get married, but they didn't know her true reasons. "I stumbled across a bit of information that may help me to achieve my goal."

"I don't understand. Did you find a way to inherit it early?"

Lilliana got up, walked to the window of the sitting room, and pulled open the curtains. She stared out at the garden and pondered how to explain what she overheard, and exactly how it fit into her idea to get everything she wanted. Various shades of roses, red, orange, and white, scattered across the garden in a pattern that reminded Lilliana of a kaleidoscope. The garden remained one of the places that she turned to when she needed to reflect on what floated through her mind. It calmed her and made it possible for her to think rationally about any issue that arose in her life. Something about being surrounded by the plant life helped her to think and form her plans with a clear head. Lilliana needed to get Gemma to aid her in her quest to leave England. They worked their magic on her as she calmly let the curtain go and turned back towards her best friend.

"I don't *ever* plan on getting married. I told you that the day we met. My parents still insisted on a season or two. They believe everyone is capable of finding love. They don't understand they are a rarity."

A sting of pain stabbed through her heart, Lilliana rubbed her chest in an attempt to erase the phantom ache. After her disastrous first season, she knew quite well how unusual it was for a love match to exist within the ton. Her choices were lecherous old men and scheming vermin only after her money. There was one man though who made her want to believe he really loved her. She found out the hard way he only wanted to use her. She was thankful he didn't achieve his goal and Lilliana came out relatively unscathed, but the damage to her belief in love sat firmly in place.

"Most matches are made for business or political

reasons. It's all about money and there is no way I'm handing over mine to a male to control."

Gemma tilted her head and crinkled her nose in confusion. Lilliana knew she didn't get it. Her friend wanted to get married and have children. The two years difference in their ages showed when they discussed the possibility of matrimony. In time, Lilliana believed Gemma would look back on this conversation with clarity. In the midst of starting her first season and barely seventeen years old, Gemma still approached life with rose-colored glasses on. For a brief moment in time Lilliana had worn that same veil of hope; her parent's love inspired her enough to want to find it herself.

Reality came crashing in like a bolt of lightning and shattered every ounce of optimism she held within her. Lilliana realized finding love at the various parties hosted within London society equaled finding a mythical creature. The chances of finding a unicorn would be an easier feat. So she gave up on love and formed a new plan for her life.

"I still think you are being preposterous. Why are you so against marriage?" Gemma folded her arms across her chest and stared at Lilliana. Her eyes pinning her in place as she spoke. "That's what a lady is expected to do after all. I just don't understand how you plan on claiming your inheritance without the benefit of a husband to help you get it."

Lilliana could feel her lips twitch into a smile. Her mother often commented on how Lilliana received all her father's traits, even his less than desirable ones. William Thorston Marsden, fifth Viscount Torrington, had a way of getting what he wanted out of people. She admired that characteristic in her father and sought to emulate it. Still, she wished she had been lucky enough to get her mother's pale blonde hair instead of her father's dark curls. In Lilliana's mind, her twin brother, Liam, was blessed because he inherited her mother's coloring.

"I suppose I should explain it so you won't be left in the dark. I'll need your assistance after all."

Gemma got up from her seat and crossed to the window where Lilliana still stood. "You're my best friend. I'll help if I can, but I'm going to be honest and say I don't like this. I don't want to lose you. Please reconsider."

"I will miss you, but I need to find my own way. Please understand this is the best thing for me."

Gemma sighed and then pulled Lilliana into her arms for a hug. Lilliana wrapped her arms around her best friend. She had been curious about Gemma once she realized who she was. Lady Gemma

Kemsley had been the girl her father wanted her brother to marry when they were younger. She sought out an introduction to get her measure and hadn't been disappointed in the young woman. They had only been friends for a few months, but in all her nineteen years she had never been close to another female her age. It didn't matter that a couple years separated their age; they were a different kind of soul mate. They appreciated each other on a level that no one else ever could or would.

"I'll try to understand. I really will, but I'm never going to like it. You are my only friend. I will always wish for you to be near me..." Gemma pulled away from Lilliana and clasped their hands together. "Tell me what I can do to help."

Lilliana knew she could count on Gemma. Elation filled her as she could envision how it would all work out. Now all she needed to do was give her all the details so she could do her part in the plan.

"I overheard my parents talking. I had no intention of listening until I heard my name spoken. I found out some interesting things that I never knew. Not the least being that Mama never intended to get married and Father had blackmailed her into agreeing to be his wife."

Gemma gasped. "What?"

"Makes you stop and question the validity of their love and all that doesn't it?"

Gemma's mouth hung open with shock radiating from her eyes. After a small pause while the information sank in she asked, "Why would he do such a thing?"

"Once upon a time Papa sailed his ship, the *Sea Rover*, as its pirate captain. Apparently he had a little feud with Mama's grandpere and she became the leverage he needed to enact his revenge. They came out of it okay, clearly as they are still together." Lilliana flipped her hand dismissively as she spoke. "The point is that Mama said that by the time I'm twenty if I still don't wish to wed, she planned on giving me the deed to the plantation in South Carolina."

Lilliana tried over and over to explain to her parents how much marriage was distasteful to her, without going into too much detail. If her father knew exactly how her heart had been bruised, he would have murderous intentions. The real issue was she didn't want anyone to know how naïve she had been. Now, she knew she could get what she wanted and nothing made her happier. Anxiety filled with equal swirls of excitement tumbled through her belly.

"That's still too long for me to wait. I won't be twenty until December and that is nine months away. What I want to do is sail there now and use my family position to gain control. My plans are not going to change just because nine months pass by."

"What good will that do? Without the deed securely in your control will they allow you to oversee the plantation? Isn't someone already there taking care of the property?" Gemma asked.

"There is an overseer yes. I'm hoping to convince him that the letter giving him orders to give me control got lost on the mail packet before my arrival. Come let's sit down in comfort as we work out the details." Lilliana grabbed Gemma's hand and led her to the settee. After they were seated she poured them both tea and handed a cup to her friend. Lilliana took a sip of tea before continuing their conversation. "I've thought a lot about what needs to be done. Even if the overseer doesn't believe I have control of the plantation no one has the authority to throw me off the property because it is owned by my family. If I have to wait, I'd rather do it in South Carolina."

Gemma nodded. "Okay, I suppose that makes sense. What do you need me to do?"

"Well the tricky part is leaving without letting my

parents know. First, I need to find a ship sailing to America. Once I book passage I'm going to need a way to get my trunks on board without raising suspicion. I'm not worried about funds. I've been saving all my pin money for months now." Lilliana gave Gemma a smile. Surely she would see how she thought of every possible issue in her plan.

"So how do you plan on getting your trunks on board the ship?"

"That is where you come in. Once I know what ship I'm on, I'd like you to invite me to come stay with you in the country for a week." Lilliana set her teacup down and gave Gemma her full attention. She really needed Gemma to help her. If she didn't, her whole plan would fall apart. Her eyes pleaded with Gemma as she spoke, "My family won't question it because they know that our schedule is relaxed at the moment. It will give me a reason to pack a trunk or two and have them loaded onto a carriage. The carriage with your family crest on it that is."

"Oh, I understand. You will have the carriage drop you off at the docks and our servants will unload your trunks to be delivered to the ship. They won't have a reason to let your family know that you're boarding the ship. The servants will assume they already know." Gemma nodded her head in understanding.

"I knew you'd get it." Excitement filled Lilliana's voice. "It's all coming together now. I only have one little facet to figure out before I can iron out the rest of the details. The first item I need to cross off my list is to figure out what ships are heading to America and if they are accepting passengers."

"However are you going to figure that out?"

"Oh, that's the easy part. I will just ask Liam," Lilliana proclaimed.

Gemma blinked several times before she asked, "Won't he find that suspicious?"

"Not at all," Lilliana said waving her hand. "He's constantly talking about the Marsden shipping line and its competitors. He just started to take over the business. Our father believes it's time for him to learn about his future inheritance."

"I see. When do you plan on getting the information out of him?"

"Tonight at the Silverton's ball. Father is making him escort me. I will make sure to have a friendly conversation with him in the carriage on our way."

"You have thought of everything. I'm sure it will work just the way you want it." A small smile grew on Gemma's face as she looked at Lilliana. "I just wish your plans didn't have to take you so far away from England. Why couldn't you have fallen in love with a nice earl or baron...or even a mere mister? Anything that might inspire you to stay where I have an actual possibility to visit you, chances are I'll never be able to travel to America to visit. Promise me you'll come back to see me."

"I promise to come back to see you. In the meantime, we'll keep in touch with lots and lots of letters. I want to know everything about your life and when you find the man of your dreams."

"Good. I suppose I should go. I'll see you tonight at the ball."

Gemma stood up and grabbed her pelisse. After she donned it, she walked over and gave Lilliana a quick hug. She watched as Gemma left the room and got up to walk back to the window to look at the rose garden. All she could do at this point was hope all of her plans went off without a hitch. Doubts clouded her mind as she knew from experience nothing ever went exactly as planned, and naught could be done to alleviate her anxiety. Lilliana decided to try and let it go. She turned and left the sitting room to find some kind of diversion. Perhaps a book would work to distract her thoughts away from any possible problems—thinking, or over thinking in her case, had always been her worst enemy. With a smile on her lips Lilliana strolled to the library. Dark feelings would not sink through and ruin her good mood. Preparation was the key to success. No one planned and schemed better than Lilliana Marsden.

CHAPTER TWO

*R*andall Collins stepped out of a black open carriage and followed the Earl of Devon into his gentleman's club, Whites. Devon wanted to discuss business in a more dignified setting, hence the journey to his favorite club. Rand didn't much like overly pompous aristocrats, but Devon had an interest in a possible investment with his shipping company. If the meeting went as planned Rand would have a new investor and could expand his business.

"Ah, here we are, have a seat Collins and we'll discuss what is next for RandCo Shipping," The Earl said as he sat down in the nearest seat at the table. "And whether or not I want to give you some of my money to invest."

It grated on his nerves he had to seek investors to expand his business. Rand had a lot of big ideas and hoped the earl liked them enough to continue to invest in shipping company. He took the seat across from the earl and settled into discussing the future of his shipping company. With a small fleet of clippers at his disposal he did well enough for himself, but wanted to branch out into steamships for larger cargos and more reliable speeds.

"Did you have a chance to look over the papers with my proposal?" Rand asked.

"I did, and I admit my knowledge of shipping is rather limited. I hope you don't mind I invited someone that knows a bit more than I do to help me decipher some of the details. Viscount Torrington and his son should arrive soon." The Earl of Devon raised his head and scanned the room. He appeared to be scanning the room, as if looking for someone he invited to join them.

Irritation filled Rand's gut as he let the earl's words absorb deep into his mind. He clenched his fists tightly under the table, not wanting the man to see how much his words bothered him. Hell yes he minded, Devon could consult anyone he chose, it was his right after all to make sure he was doing the right thing for himself. However, he could have at least let Rand know they'd be meeting with someone else prior to arriving at the club. It was hard to be prepared for a meeting when all of the details hadn't been presented in advance. Before he could voice objection, two men walked in and took a seat at the table. One was as dark as the other was light. They bore a striking resemblance, in spite of the opposite coloring, that made Rand believe them to be closely related.

"Ah Torrington glad you and Liam could make it," Devon said. "This here is Randall Collins. He has grand ideas for steamships. What are your thoughts on the matter?"

As they had not been introduced, Rand gathered the older gentleman Devon spoke to was Torrington, the man he previously mentioned would be joining them. The upper class tended to refer to each other by their titles or last names. Rand couldn't wait until he could sail back to America. The higher born in English society had a snobbish attitude that he had trouble stomaching. Torrington nodded his head at both Rand and Devon before he started to speak, "Liam knows a bit more about steamships than I do. He has been looking into them for a while now to determine if they are worth investing in. I'm a clipper man, but I realize their days are numbered."

"I like the idea of steamships, but even they have their pitfalls. The coal needed to keep them running can be expensive. The cargo needs to bring in a more than fair price if a profit is to be made. They have their advantages, faster and more reliable travel. I think it's more economical for most cargo to continue to be brought over by clipper. Steamships are great for passengers and mail." The light haired man nodded at them as he sat up straight and looked Rand directly in the eye as he delivered his viewpoint.

It was obvious that Liam's beliefs were in direct opposition to his own. Rand clenched his hands into tight fists underneath the table as anger and frustration permeated his whole body. The boy probably had a point, although minute, Rand however did not want to deal in passenger ships. People made things messy. They could be demanding and irritating on a good day and damn abusive any other time. The chances of him being willing to start a passenger line bordered on slim to none.

"Is that the only good thing you can think of for steamships? What about cargo that requires a faster delivery? I know you English favor your tea. Steamships travel at faster speeds and allows for a swifter arrival. This means what you deem to be important cargo will arrive to its destination much sooner." He had to gain control of the conversation before these idiots talked Devon out of investing in his shipping line.

Steamships did make great passenger ships. The mail packets arrived much faster when they were placed on a ship powered by steam, but Rand had grander ideas. There were plenty of reasons to start investing in steamships. Those that began to do it sooner would have profits much sooner than those waiting to see if it worked. Sometimes it was worth it to take on a risky venture; although Rand didn't think it was as chancy as they were making it sound.

A bit of color formed on Liam's face. He clearly didn't like pointing out flaws in his estimation of the value of steamships. "You make a valid point, sir. Some cargo could benefit from the faster steamship. There is a clipper design that has been noted to bypass even a faster steamship. The record for the ship surpassed the fourteen knots of the steamship. That clipper managed to snatch up some of the tea trade. We had a few ships built around that design and they have worked wonderfully with any cargo that requires a more speedy arrival." Liam continued to glare at him as he spoke. His eyes crunched up in disapproval and his lips pursed into a thin line.

"Okay, I admit I'm just getting more confused the more these two gentlemen talk. Tell me straight Torrington, are steamships a good investment?" Devon asked.

"The short answer is yes, and no." Torrington grinned.

Torrington had an amused smile on his face as he watched his son sit back in displeasure. Apparently Liam's attitude entertained him or it could be the volley of their conversation back and forth, Rand didn't care to know what that something was though. He just wanted to derail them before they ruined his investment possibility. Damn them and their advice. If they kept talking about the negativities surrounding steamships they were going to talk the earl out of investing, and Rand would be right back where he started.

"That doesn't bloody help me." Devon threw his hands up in frustration.

"That's because there isn't an easy answer to your question. Any new venture is risky. All signs point to steamships eventually taking over. There are a few ships that are built to be powered by both steam and wind. We are having a few of those built to try out in our shipping line." Liam rested his hand on the table and tapped his forefinger on the polished wood as he explained, "The idea is that if coal runs out or becomes too expensive the option to use wind is still available and not all will be lost in the voyage. It will probably be a few years before we branch into a ship completely powered by steam."

"So you both do not believe steamships are the sound investment right now?" Heat began to dissipate through Rand as his anger reached a boiling point.

"In the future yes, but now it is still risky," Torrington said. "They are making a lot of progress in their designs, but they all have flaws. I'd go with what is a known quantity."

Rand unclenched his fists and wiped his sweaty palms over his thighs. His lips pursed in displeasure as he considered how to proceed. He couldn't erase the irritation from his voice as he spoke. "And yet you are still willing to try out a glorified clipper ship that could also be powered by steam?"

"Yes." Torrington continued with a bit of mockery in his voice, "I did say I leaned towards clippers at the beginning of the conversation."

Damned Englishman, and their perverse ways. The conversation was spiraling out of control. Rand tried to steer the conversation in the direction he wanted, but they were relentless in their opinions.

He curled his fingers into fists underneath the table and refrained from smashing them against the polished wood.

"I'll admit there is a certain beauty about clippers, but let's be realistic. The popularity of the ship has faded a lot over the past twenty years. The ship isn't seen in quite the same light as it used to be."

"So do you recommend investing or not?" Devon asked as he turned his attention once more on Torrington. "I need to give the man an answer."

Torrington looked at Devon and shrugged his shoulders. He looked him directly in the eyes as he spoke. "Honestly, it's up to you and how much of a risk you are willing to take with your money. It isn't a bad investment. No matter what, eventually you will make money." Torrington picked up his drink and took a quick swig. He set his glass back on the table and scanned the table before his eyes landed on the Earl. "To put it simply, Devon, it depends on the market and how well the cargo is managed. I did look over his plan and RandCo has been steadily gaining in capital. It just hasn't been at a rapid pace. Expanding at this juncture requires more money and it's not gaining enough on its own."

The more they opened their mouths the more irritated Rand became. He couldn't believe the gall of these men. They were talking around him instead of including him in the conversation. He had to force his way into it in order to be heard. He built RandCo all on his own. Yes, the progress had crawled at the pace of a snail, but the growth remained true. It might take him longer than he wanted it to, but he could continue to do it on his own. He'd be damned if he remained sitting here taking their distain and disapproval.

Rand forced his way into the conversation. "Good of you to give the stamp of approval on my business, Ol' Chap. Why don't I save you all the time and just say that the offer is off the table. I don't especially like being discussed like I'm not here."

Liam began, "We didn't mean to imply—"

Rand interrupted, "Save it. You act like I don't know a lick about business. I built this company all on my own without your expert advice. I can continue to assemble it without your money too, Devon. I admit the boost probably would have made expanding easier. I just don't like the strings that extra help apparently comes with."

He looked over and found Torrington studying him as if trying to ascertain his origin. He must not have a lot of experience dealing with Americans. He knew he could be a bit brash and defensive at times, but he had no desire to change.

"A bit hot-headed, aren't you." Torrington raised his eyebrows at him and a quirky smile lifted at the corners of his mouth.

"A product of where I happened to be raised, I suppose." Rand shrugged.

Torrington laughed before saying, "In America? Yeah, I suppose that could be the explanation. From my experience most of you could take a bit of lessons on diplomacy."

"And you all could learn to be more accepting of the differences in all men," Rand retorted.

"Down puppy. I meant no offense. My wife happens to be American. She can be a bit...stubborn at times. Don't do anything rash," Torrington reasoned.

Rand had to admit that little tidbit amused him some. Torrington's wife must be an exceptional woman to put up with his arrogance on a daily basis. It would be interesting to meet her and get a more in depth look at her character. "Your wife's American? What state did she hail from? Maybe I know her family."

"Doubtful as they all died a number of years ago. Her plantation is being run by an overseer at present. It's located in Charleston, South Carolina."

"I never knew that," Devon stated.

"Yes, we're lucky it survived the War Between the States. She left shortly before the war broke out and sailed to France to live with her grandpere," Torrington explained.

"How ever did your plantation manage to survive the war?" Rand had to admit that he found it interesting that they had a plantation in Charleston that survived the war. A lot of the plantations had been burned to the ground by the Union army.

"Luck mostly." Torrington leaned back in his chair. "The union army decided to use it as a hospital. My wife, Pia, told her overseer to remain as neutral as possible and that allowed for a certain amount of leniency from both sides of the conflict."

"Well if we're done discussing business how about a bit of pleasure?" Devon asked.

"What do you have in mind?" Torrington questioned as he leaned forward and rested his hands on the table. "I have plans with my wife this evening and can't be drawn into anything too extensive."

"How about a game of whist?" Devon asked.

"I have to be back in a couple hours to take Lily to that ball." Liam looked at his father as he spoke.

Torrington nodded. "Good point. Lily has a temper and she isn't afraid to use it. Best if you're not late. Why don't you take the carriage home and send it back for me."

"I can always give you a lift back, Torrington," Devon offered. "Although I'm supposed to go to that blasted ball tonight too. Gemma is expecting me to escort her."

"As much as I hate to admit it, I think we'll have to attempt more amusing pursuits at a later date. Maybe tomorrow night?" Torrington looked to Devon for confirmation.

"Splendid idea." Devon nodded his affirmation. He turned towards Rand and asked, "Collins, you want to go to the ball?"

"Can't say I've ever been to a ball before. Sounds fun. I have a few days before I sail back home. It could be a nice diversion." Rand had been watching them discuss their options for entertainment. It resembled a pugilist in the ring; they volleyed shots back and forth at each other and danced around any real issues. If he hadn't been so irritated, he'd be a bit more fascinated by their way of speaking to each other. He never had any desire to go to a ball before, but he could add it to his once in a lifetime experiences.

"Good, good. Then just come with me to my townhouse. My valet can help you get ready and you can help me escort my daughter, Gemma."

Rand got up to follow the earl out of his club. He nodded at Torrington and Liam. "Nice meeting you gentlemen. Perhaps we'll see more of each other before I depart."

Pompous jerks. His real wishes didn't even come close to wanting to see them ever again. He knew he'd see them at the ball later that evening, but hoped it would be the last time he ever laid eyes on them. They single-handedly made him restructure his whole plan for expanding his business. He didn't hold them in any high esteem. The meeting did not go as he intended it to. These men and their grand ideas, or lack thereof, had made sure of that. No, what he felt for them bordered on hate. He had to deal with uppity men who believed they were better than him his whole life. A person didn't grow up in an orphanage without having some lasting internal scars. The emotional distress the high class brought out was deep rooted and he couldn't let go of it easily. In his experience they didn't give a damn for anyone, but themselves. These individuals were not different. If he never saw them again he might be able to forget their existence.

CHAPTER THREE

*L*illiana sat down at her vanity table and put the finishing touches on her hair. She did very well getting herself ready without a maid of her own. Having to depend on anyone for assistance went against all of her ideals. She had been ordering dresses that were easy to put on herself since before her come out ball three years prior. It had taken her a while to learn how to do her own hair, but like anything she put her mind to she excelled at it. Today, she wrapped her ebony curls partially up in a chignon with a few curls falling down to frame her face. Satisfied with her handi-work, Lilliana stood up and stepped into black satin shoes. She stopped wearing light colors when she decided never to marry. Young girls wore pastels.

While they didn't have much choice in the matter, she certainly did.

Society dictated that if a lady remained unmarried they needed to appear more demure. One of the ways to convey that distinction to the world was in the color of their dresses. A year ago Lilliana decided she that she would no longer wear such hideous colors. White and pink did nothing for her complexion. She needed bolder colors that enhanced her looks. So she convinced her mother to allow her to wear something more suited for her. After a long heated debate she won and had more flattering colors for her wardrobe. She reached down and smoothed the skirt of her cobalt ball gown. The blue gown enhanced the color of her eyes and enhanced their appeal. She had fallen in love with the color and fabric when she visited the modiste a few weeks ago. It made her happy to be able to finally show off the creation at a ball.

Lilliana loved to dress up and attend parties. It made her feel special and beautiful. Not to mention how fun it was to be able to dance and laugh with her friend, Gemma. She may not want a husband, but she still knew how to enjoy herself within the expectations set by the ton.

Lilliana grabbed her gloves and left the room.

She walked down the stairs just as her brother walked in the door.

"Oh good, you're ready to go," Liam said.

"Did you doubt I would be?" Lilliana raised her eyebrows at her brother. "I'm always prompt and you know it."

They were twins, not that you could tell by looking at them. They each had very distinct features. Lilliana looked at Liam noting how much his coloring favored their mother. She couldn't help wishing once again she favored her mother instead of her father. They may each take after a different parent, but one thing remained true; a Marsden didn't take it well when someone ordered them around. Liam had a more diplomatic personality, but even he had bursts of temper. Liam managed to hold on and fight battles he believed were worth the energy needed to expend in order to win them. When he happened to be in a rage though, it was best to clear the room because he exploded when he couldn't hold his anger in.

"I'm aware of your tenacious attitude. I'm always prepared for a battle when I have to deal with you," Liam declared.

"Nonsense. I'm the epitome of graciousness." Lilliana flashed Liam a wholly wicked, gamine smile.

At her pronouncement Liam began to laugh. His chuckles bounced over the walls and boomed loudly throughout the entrance hall. The color of his face became bright red as he gasped for breath. Lilliana moved past him to wear her pelisse hung by the door. Early spring in London still held a chill, and she didn't want to be cold as they traveled to the ball. After she had the pelisse securely around her shoulders, she turned back to her brother. His laugher slowed down to a light gurgle as if he attempted to rein it in.

"I don't see what you find so funny, little brother."

"You are never gracious. You're a demanding wench, and you know it," Liam retorted.

Ignoring him, Lilliana strolled towards the entranceway. They walked out of the front door and into the awaiting carriage. Lilliana waited for her brother to be seated before she replied to his taunt. No reason not to be comfortable for the upcoming disagreement.

"No need to be mean, I can be nice. " Lilliana tilted her head. "If it serves my purpose."

"Lily dear, you don't do nice. You scheme and cajole your way into everything. No worries, I love you and wouldn't have you any other way. It's part of your charm." Liam flashed her a smile that mirrored hers. He could look positively wicked at times.

"You're just trying to suck up now for acting like a bird-wit."

"Awe, that's a bit harsh. I'm never thoughtless. You know that," Liam told her.

"Then explain your actions just now?" Lilliana raised her eyebrows in question."Cause you generally don't act like an arse."

"I met an interesting American today. His comments grated on me a bit."

Lilliana's interest piqued at his comment. She couldn't tip her hand too much, or he'd latch on to her questioning and ask some relentless ones of his own. They were fairly close and often sensed things about each other. Liam knew her too well and probably would figure out before anyone else what her actual plans were. She couldn't allow that to happen for any reason. He would do everything he could to stop her from traveling to South Carolina.

Besides leaving Gemma, she would miss Liam a great deal. If anyone could persuade her to abandon her plans, it was her brother. So she began her questions remaining as neutral as possible.

"What did he do to irritate you so much?"

"I can't pinpoint it exactly. I think it was basically centered around his attitude. He had a penchant for rudeness."

"Sounds like an interesting chap. Any chance I can meet him?" Lilliana inquired.

"For what purpose? You aren't going to start some kind of feud with him because he was annoying, are you?" Liam questioned.

"Please." Lilliana raised her eyebrows. "What kind of person do you take me for?"

"The kind that enjoys trouble a bit too much."

Liam did have a point—she enjoyed getting people riled. She often said things just to see what kind of reaction she could get out to them. It amused her to no end how often they fell for it. This time though she really did want to meet the American. He must have arrived in England by way of ship and chances were he'd know the next ship sailing back home.

"You know me too well. I don't like people that aggravate my family in any way." Lilliana agreed.

"No worries, he didn't bother me that much," Liam replied, "but if you really want to meet him then you will have a chance tonight."

"Really? Why is that?"

This was going rather easy. Almost too effortless, and maybe she should take that into consideration, but Lilliana believed in taking risks. She needed to know why he was going to be at the ball. Any information about him would be useful in gaining his trust and help in obtaining the necessary sailing schedule.

"He is the guest of the Earl of Devon. He is attending the ball tonight with his family."

"Oh, poor Gemma."

"What the bloody hell does Gemma have to do with it?" Liam inquired.

"Well, isn't it obvious? As the guest of her father she'll have to put up with his rotten attitude more than we will." Lilliana explained.

"I'm sure your friend will be just fine. If not, you will come to her rescue like you always do."

"I don't get why you don't like her that much. She is the sweetest girl. You should try and get to know her a bit."

Lilliana could see Liam's frustration as he ran his hands over his face. No doubt learning the business had started to take its toll on him. She knew their father could be demanding and expected a lot out of his children. Perhaps she should go a bit easier on him. His stress levels had taken an all-time high when he started to take on more responsibility. He needed to learn it all so that one day he'd be in a position to take control.

Lilliana wanted to believe her parents were infallible, but she knew that someday they would no longer be with them. Their father realized it all too well. He lost his parents at a young age and hadn't been prepared to run the business on his own. So for that reason he started to teach Liam everything he needed to know as early as possible. Viscount Torrington didn't want his son to be taken by surprise with the responsibility of the estate and many businesses in his holdings.

"I'm sure she is delightful. I don't have time for her kind of amiable right now." Liam stared at her with derision in his eyes as the sarcastic reply left his lips. Something about Gemma bothered him, but Lilliana didn't know what. He always seemed to want to avoid her and he made every attempt to do so.

"What's that supposed to mean?" Lilliana asked. She sat up and stared at her brother anger simmering through her, making her cheeks feel heated. It offended her that he found Gemma so unworthy.

"Don't take that tone with me. Nothing against

her, but you know she wants to get married. I see the stars in her eyes and I'm not that guy. I wish she'd quit looking at me like that. It will be a number of years before I even consider getting leg-shackled."

Oh, she got it all right. Her friend didn't compare to his expectations, and somehow he had gotten the notion she sought his attention. Maybe he saw something she didn't when looking at Gemma or it could be he was projecting his own ideas onto her friend. It might not have anything specifically to do with Gemma, but more what she represented to him. Liam had a lot on his mind and marriage didn't top his list of priorities. Lilliana didn't think that Gemma had set her sights on any one in particular. Sure, her brother exhibited a handsome face, but even Gemma had to realize his youth played a part in his reluctance to get married.

"I'm sure you're wrong about her. Yes, she does want to get married. She looks at everyone. You're around me a lot as my chaperone and she'd be a fool not to notice you. Nothing more than that." Lilliana flipped her hand *nonchalantly*. "I know you have your own resentments, but you have to remember she didn't have anything to do with what our two fathers originally planned. Besides, she hasn't settled on anyone just yet." Lilliana looked into his eyes pinning him with a glare. "Be nice."

The carriage stopped, and Lilliana looked up to see a footman holding the door open. They finally arrived at the Silverton ball. It was now time to start putting her plan in motion.

"I'm not going to argue with you, Lily. Let's try to have some fun at this function tonight," Liam suggested.

Lilliana smiled at his offer of peace. "I don't want to argue any more than you do. Let's go inside and see who's in town to enjoy this ball." She planned on having lots of fun at the social gathering. The first thing she wanted to do involved garnering an introduction to her brother's American foe.

They stepped out of the carriage and walked up the steps to enter the Silverton residence. Lady Silverton always hosted the best balls each season; Lilliana hoped that this one proved to be just as wonderful as the ones she had attended in the past. She knew at the very least she'd be a step further in her plans to go to America by the end of the ball. She hoped that the man she sought out could answer all of her questions.

"By the way what is the name of the American that you didn't like too much?" Lilliana asked.

"Why? I thought you decided to leave him be?" Liam asked.

"I never agreed to any such thing. I need to make sure he is an okay fellow to be around Gemma."

"Ah I see, I suppose that makes a bit of sense. His name is Randall Collins."

"Good to know. I like to have as much information as possible before I meet someone."

"I'm surprised you're not interrogating me for more details."

"Why? Is there something else I should know?"

"Nothing I can think of. I doubt you will have to worry very much though," Liam replied.

"Don't concern yourself with what I worry about, but why do you believe I won't have to?" she asked.

"He owns his own shipping line. He said he only planned on being in England a few more days before he set sail for home."

That had to be the best news that she'd hear that night. Lilliana carefully schooled her face to remain blank. She didn't want to give away how much his statement excited her. He owned his own ships! Surely she could talk him into allowing her passage on one of them. Lilliana wanted to rub her hands together with glee, but knew the action would only raise more questions. It took everything she had to physically restrain herself from making her hands do the motions.

"Oh good. Maybe I'll leave the man alone then."

"Somehow I doubt you will," Liam muttered.

"You have no faith in me."

"I have lots of confidence in you," Liam told her. "I just also happen to know you too well."

"I know." She sighed. "If you want you can go find one of your friends to talk to, I'll be fine. I'm going to probably be with Gemma all night anyway."

They walked into the ballroom after they were announced. Liam scanned the room and spotted someone he wanted to talk to. He nodded at them and strolled over to their side. Lilliana scoured the ballroom looking for her best friend. Drat, it looks like they haven't arrived yet. She'd have to bide her time and remain calm until she got her chance to accost Randall Collins for information. She walked to a chair and sat to await their arrival. She tapped her fingers on the arm of the chair. Many people believed that patience was a virtue, but the concept escaped Lilliana. She never did understand why she should be made to wait. Perhaps her actions could be construed as spoiled, but she liked to think of them as exacting and necessary. The night would be long if she had to sit here anxious for the Devon party to arrive. The American captain held the final detail to tie it all together. He needed to arrive and soon. If his ship held the capabilities to transport her to her desired destination, she'd unleash all her charm on the man. He wouldn't know what hit him. Lilliana always got what she wanted.

CHAPTER FOUR

"Ah we're here," the Earl of Devon said. "The worst part about these functions is waiting in line to get out of the carriage."

Rand agreed with the earl's assessment. Nothing compared to the atrocious confinement he'd been subjected to with the earl who talked too much and his daughter who could barely string two words together.

"Well at least we can finally get out of the carriage and stretch our legs," Rand said.

They each stepped out of the carriage and walked up the steps. Rand followed the earl and his daughter as they entered the residence. So far he believed the choice to attend the ball ranked near the top of his list of his worst decisions. He hoped his opinion of the situation proved to be wrong once he actually made it inside and experienced the event itself. After the announcement of their arrival, they walked down into the elaborate ballroom. It appeared as if anyone and everyone had shown up for the ball. The possibility they were amongst the last to arrive occurred to Rand as he tried to follow the earl and his daughter through the crowd. Once they got to the far side of the ballroom, they stopped walking and turned to look at the guests dancing on the ballroom floor.

"Quite the turnout, isn't it?" a voice asked from behind Rand. He turned to see a beautiful woman with black curls floating around her heart-shaped face. Her full lips formed a crimson bow as they tilted up into a pleasant smile. For a brief moment he stood still, stunned at her appearance. In those brief moments he realized the lovely young woman came over to speak to the earl's daughter.

"Oh good, I thought it would prove impossible to find you in the crush of people here." Gemma gave the girl a quick hug.

A lighthearted laugh floated from within her and it seared Rand's soul. The night improved considerably with her appearance. Maybe the decision to come hadn't been the worst one he'd ever made after all...

"You doubt me?" she asked. "What is it with people doubting my abilities tonight, first my brother, and now you. Have faith in me please."

"Of course not! I would never doubt you. It just took us forever to arrive. I despaired at the idea I might not be able to spend any time with you. Have you danced yet?" Gemma inquired.

"Yes, I have danced. You know my card doesn't stay empty for very long, I have lots of names on my card. It's nearly full." She waved her card at Gemma with a triumphant grin on her face.

Rand stood there waiting for the forgetful chit to introduce him to her lovely friend. He hoped to add his name to her dance card before it filled up. By her last statement he believed he would be too late unless he acted fast, he prayed she would agree to add his name to her card. Her eyes glanced over and locked with his.

"Do I know you?" she asked.

"Oh how rude of me. I'm sorry I should have introduced you." Gemma apologized.

Yeah, she should have. Her youth exploded out of her every time she opened her mouth. Hopefully she matured as she got older. Otherwise her future husband may have an annoying female to deal with. She didn't matter to him though, his eyes remained glued on her friend.

"Mr. Randall Collins." Gemma gestured toward him. "Please meet Miss Lilliana Marsden."

Finally a name to go with the beautiful creature! It suited her perfectly. Her features rivaled any lily he had ever had the pleasure to see. Indeed, she was an elegant flower expertly cultivated and pleasing to be around. He really needed to hold her in his arms even for a brief moment. The introductions were made perhaps now he could entertain the possibility of dancing with her.

"Nice to meet you, Miss Marsden," he said.

"The pleasure is all mine, Mr. Collins," Lilliana replied. "You're not from around here are you?"

"No I'm not, I'm actually from America. South Carolina to be exact," Rand explained.

"Really? That's interesting. Lilliana has ties to South Carolina." Gemma jumped into the conversation as she relayed that interesting tidbit of information.

Rand turned his attention to Gemma and stared at her with little interest. He had forgotten the little mouse still stood by them. As soon as he had Lilliana's attention, Gemma became nonexistent.

Her father had abandoned them both a while ago; Rand had no clue where the earl had disappeared too.

"I didn't know that, but of course we did just meet," Rand replied. "Where in South Carolina do you have ties?" Rand turned his attention back to the enchanting Lilliana.

"Charleston. Do you reside near there?" she responded.

"I actually reside in a nearby town, Beaufort."

"Oh, that's lovely. I have only visited South Carolina once. We sailed over when I was a child to check on the property held by my family. I'd like to see it again someday." Lilliana's voice had a whimsical tone as she spoke. A faraway expression clouded her eyes as she appeared deep in thought. After a few moments she shook her head and gave her attention back to Rand. "Are you sailing back soon?" she asked.

"In a few days I am heading home," he replied. "There hasn't been a whole lot in England to inspire me to stay."

"Nonsense." Lilliana smiled. "There's a lot in England that is absolutely stunning. You're just not inclined to give it a chance."

Rand found himself smiling back at her, absolutely enchanted. A more charming female did not exist, at least one he had ever met. He must dance with her soon. Rand really needed to garner any chance he could to touch her, no matter how brief.

"I heard you say that your dance card had yet to be filled. Any chance I can add my name to it?" he requested.

"Oh." Lilliana looked at her card and chewed on her bottom lip. "I don't know I had hoped to spend some time with Gemma."

"Please." His eyes begged her to accept.

"Oh, all right, let's see. I suppose you can have the next dance. It's a waltz. Is that okay?"

"I have no problem with that," he agreed.

A half-smile formed on his face. He couldn't have been happier with the outcome if he tried, and a waltz would allow him to touch her more that he had hoped to. He couldn't wait to hold her in his arms and have her full attention.

"Gemma, you don't mind, do you?" she turned and asked her friend. "Maybe you can find a dance partner too."

As if on cue a male walked up behind Lilliana and said, "Are you staying out of trouble, imp?"

Rand looked up to see his nemesis from the earlier business meeting standing by Lilliana. He had no clue who Liam actually addressed with his statement until Lilliana spoke.

"Oh bother," Lilliana's annoyance came to the surface with her statement. "I'm being good. Go find someone else to interrogate." Lilliana grabbed his arm to prevent him from leaving. "No better yet stay. You can dance with Gemma. She needs a partner for the next dance."

Liam looked disturbed at the idea of dancing with Gemma. Not that Rand could blame him either. Given the choice he'd choose Lilliana every time. The little mouse seemed to become even more demure in his the presence of Liam Marsden. She withdrew and appeared both happy and frustrated to have him in her presence. If Rand had more time he would probably wonder why she was displaying such a huge contradiction, but at that particular moment he really didn't care.

"Uh...sure, I guess I can."

"You don't have to." Gemma leaped into the conversation to dismiss the idea. "I know you don't like to dance."

"No, it's okay. I want to," Liam said.

Rand didn't believe him for a minute. He concluded Liam only placated the girl. Not for a second did he think the young man actually *wanted* to dance with Lady Gemma. A look of fear crossed over Liam's features before he masked it with a more congenial expression. He didn't care though because he got what he wanted out of the situation. Lilliana Marsden would soon be in his arms. Rand only thing he cared about getting her there.

Lilliana stepped up and placed a kiss on Liam's cheek just as the sounds of the music of the current dance ended. She had a bright smile on her face and her eyes glowed with happiness. "Oh, that's fantastic. I knew I could count on you."

Rand felt irritation grow inside of him at the sight of Liam, but he let it go as soon as Lilliana turned towards him and held out her hand for him to take in his. This was what he had been waiting for since the moment he turned to see her for the first time.

"I suppose that means it's time for the next dance," Rand stated.

"You're going to dance with him?" Liam scowled. "I'm not sure that's a good idea."

"I don't care what your opinion is, Liam," Lilliana said. "I want to dance and Mr. Collins offered. Go dance with Gemma and quit being a brooding chaperone."

He glared at her, but then turned towards

Gemma and took her hands. Rand still holding Lilliana's hand in the crook of his arm led her out to the dance floor. Gemma and Liam followed them, and they began the waltz. Lilliana danced beautifully in his arms. She had a light step and floated around the ballroom floor.

"Can I ask you a question?" Inquisitiveness reflected in her eyes as she stared directly into his. She mesmerized him and held his attention captive with her own.

"You can ask me anything."

"Is it possible for me to sail back to South Carolina with you?"

"Pardon me?" Rand stared at her with befuddlement.

"I want to go live on our plantation in Charleston. My father is being difficult about it. I decided I would have to take matters into my own hands," Lilliana explained.

In that moment he realized exactly who she happened to be related to. It all clicked into place as he saw Liam dance by with Gemma in his arms. Lilliana Marsden and Liam were brother and sister. So that made her the daughter of Viscount Torrington. Rand knew he would regret it if he allowed her on his ship. The little he garnered about the man while he sat before him in the business meeting earlier told him a lot about the man. He had very high expectations and little time for dimwits. No doubt he would kill him for taking his daughter away from him. Liam, her devoted brother, would help his father accomplish the task.

"I'm not so sure that is a good idea." He looked down at her with wariness in his eyes. "Your father is a force of nature and your brother isn't far behind him."

"I don't care. I'm capable of making my own decisions."

"And you expect me to take on their wrath?" Amusement laced his voice. "I'm not sure I'm up to these lofty expectations you have for me."

"Absolutely." She wrinkled her nose up at him. "I think you're more than up for what I'm asking of you."

"So you actually want me to help you run away from home?"

"Well, when you put it like that... Yes, I do."

He would be every kind of fool to go along with her idea, yet he wanted to. If he took her with him he might have a possibility of winning her over. In England he didn't stand a chance in hell of getting her to accept him as her own. As soon as he laid eyes on her he knew he wanted her. The more he talked with her the more he liked the idea of holding on to her forever. As foolish as her idea appeared to be Rand knew it also happened to be the only opportunity he may get of actually having her.

"I suppose you have all of the necessary details worked out," he replied. "I'm not likely to have your male relations storm my ship and demand you back before we depart am I?"

"Trust me. I'm good at strategies. You just happen to be the last detail I needed to make it all work the way I wanted."

"Trust has nothing to do with it." Rand laughed. "It has more to do with self-preservation. I happen to fancy breathing."

"Don't be ridiculous," Lilliana retorted. "There isn't any reason to be so dramatic. My father isn't likely to kill you."

"Right. Because he is the personification of civility."

He watched her blink several times as his words sank in. How bad of a temper did Viscount Torrington actually have? Rand watched as she mulled over his words. Perhaps he had misunderstood the viscount. His impression of the man suggested he had a violent side. One he had no problem showing to the world if he deemed it necessary.

"Father does have a temper, but I still believe you have nothing to worry about," Lilliana explained.

"You said I happened to be the final detail in your plans." Rand sighed. "Were you waiting for me to show up?"

What were the chances the chit new of his existence before their introduction? No, it wasn't likely as he hadn't been in England that long.

"Not exactly, I had no clue you existed before today," she told him. "These plans have been in the works for a few weeks now."

"And yet I'm the very thing you need to make it all work. How is that possible?"

"Simple really, I need someone with a ship that is willing to transport me. I am hoping that person is you."

He wondered how far he could push her. The decision to give into her and take her on his ship had already been made. Lilliana just didn't know he already decided to let her come back to America with him, but only because it worked in his own plans.

"What do I get for my trouble?" he asked. "I'd be risking quite a lot to assist you with your scheme."

"What do you want? Money? I certainly can afford to pay for my passage."

Rand's lips rose into a cocky smile. He desired a lot from her, but at this point only one thing would do as payment. Would the lovely lady be willing to give it to him? He had nothing to lose and only one way to find out.

"How about a kiss?"

Lilliana looked stunned as she stared unblinkingly at him, and then just as suddenly she stopped dancing right in the middle of the dance floor. Her face flushed a pretty shade of pink as she began to move to the music again with him in the lead.

"How forward of you. I'm not sure I like your idea of compensation."

"It's a small thing, one little kiss. To be given to me at a time of my choosing." He leaned in close to her and whispered in her ear. "Are you afraid?"

Lilliana's breath sucked deep into her chest, and he could feel her slowly exhale it in little pants. Her pulse raced on her wrist beneath the palm of his hand and thrummed a small beat as he held it firmly in his grasp. A blush formed on her cheeks turning them a nice shade of pink, and her lips parted in anticipation. Her body's reactions suggested she had an interest in kissing him also. Would she take the

DAWN BROWER

bait and give him what he desired? He needed her to accept the proposal. Once she did he'd have her sailing with him in a few short days.

"All right, you have a deal," she agreed.

"Excellent. I will send information on where you can board the ship. I look forward to our voyage together."

He led her back to the side of the room when the dance ended and stopped next to her brother and Gemma. She looked up at him and smiled before turning her attention back to her friend. Rand nodded at Liam and sauntered away. He had some preparations to make before he could welcome her on his ship. Tonight, it looked like he was going to be preparing his ship to sail a tad earlier than he originally planned. Oh, but what an extraordinary reason to go through the hassle of making the trip a bit prematurely. He couldn't wait to have Lilliana Marsden on his ship, and in his world.

CHAPTER FIVE

*L*illiana couldn't believe how easy everything started to fall into place. A note from Randall Collins arrived early that morning. His plans to leave had changed slightly. Instead of three days, his ship would sail back to North Carolina the next day. Excitement filled her as she realized it had all worked out as she planned. Randall Collins, with his unruly dark brown hair and mischievous hazel eyes, took her breath away. She didn't want to agree to a kiss as payment, but at the same time she anticipated it. He stirred feelings in her that she didn't know how to explain. So she decided to push it out of her mind. A lot needed to be done before she could leave with him.

She sent a note to Gemma to come visit her for

tea so she could wrap up that little detail. Gemma
needed to be made aware of when her invitation to
visit happened to be taking place. She also needed to
get permission from her parents to stay a week or
two at the Earl of Devon's country estate. Her father
would be the hardest to persuade, so he sat on the
top of her list of things to accomplish that day. She
left her bedroom and walked down the stairs to his
study. No time like the present to get that little tidbit
checked of her to do list.

"Are you busy?" She knocked on the side of the
doorframe and walked into her father's study.

Viscount Torrington sat behind his desk with a
bunch of papers scattered across the top of it. His
long dark hair tapered at the nape of his neck, but a
riotous strand escaped and folded over the top of his
forehead. His head rose at the sound of her voice
and his blue eyes twinkled with delight.

"For my favorite daughter? Absolutely not." Her
father rose to greet her.

"I'm your only daughter." A tiny giggle escaped
her mouth as she crossed the room to give him
a hug.

"That's a good thing too," he retorted. "I don't
know if I could've handled two of you."

"Of course you could have." Lilliana gave him a mischievous grin. "I'm the essence of all that is good."

"Are you trying to trick me?" Viscount Torrington laughed. "I'm made of sterner stuff than those other fools you walk all over. What do I owe the pleasure of this visit?"

"Nothing much really, Gemma has to go back to her family's country estate for a week or two. She invited me to join her. It's my hope you'll allow me to go."

"I don't know if that's the best idea right now, Lily. Things are a bit busy around here at the moment," he explained.

"That's exactly why you should allow me to visit. Liam is busy learning the business. You can't expect him to keep escorting me to these functions. It's only the little season anyway. I don't need to go and it'll be nice to spend time with Gemma."

"What does your mother have to say?" he asked.

"I haven't spoken to her yet. I figured I'd approach you first. Please Daddy, let me go." Lilliana used her most coaxing voice on her father. She stuck her bottom lip out in a mock pout and batted her eyelashes at him expectantly.

"Thor, are you busy?" They turned as they heard a

voice from behind them. "Oh, I didn't know you were in here Lily."

Her mother either had the worst timing or the best. Lady Torrington strolled into the room with a questioning look on her face. Her pale blonde hair was perfectly coifed without a hair out of place, and her emerald green gown rustled as she made her way across the room to join her husband and daughter. Lilliana took a moment to envy her mother's beauty and wished once again she had been blessed with her coloring. Sometimes she hated her brother for getting the lucky genes. She could very well deter her father from allowing her to go to Gemma's. If only she had more time to talk to him before her mother interrupted. She needed to convince her father to allow her to visit Gemma's country estate. Her mother's timing may have interrupted her plans, but maybe she could salvage it somehow.

"Hello Mama," Lilliana said. "I stopped in to ask Father's permission to visit with Gemma at her family's country estate for a week."

"Oh? And when were you going to ask me?" her mother asked.

"After I finished talking with Father," Lilliana said.

"Pia, I just asked her if she already spoke with

you," her father said. "I think it would be okay for her to have a small visit. As long as she isn't gone more than a week."

Lilliana could feel elation soaring through her. She rocked on her heels and hugged herself with joy. Apparently that small amount of time had been enough to convince her father to allow her to go. Thank God for small favors. She needed to be on that ship in the morning.

"I suppose that would be fine," her mother said. "When will you be leaving?"

"Tomorrow morning. The earl's carriage is going to stop by and pick me up. It's short notice I know, it's why I'm asking now so I can get my trunks packed."

"All right, I don't like that you are leaving so fast, but I guess I'm find it to be acceptable. Our social functions are pretty slim right now anyway," her mother said.

Lilliana threw her arms around her mother in a fierce hug. She loved her parents dearly, but they tended to be a bit overprotective. It shamed her to know that her leaving would hurt them, but she had to leave, her happiness depended on it. She truly believed she belonged in South Carolina.

"Thank you, Mama. I need the break and some

quiet time with Gemma."

"What I don't get a hug?" her father asked.

"You already got a hug," Lilliana teased.

"What I don't rate a second one?" He raised his eyebrows at her statement.

"Of course you do," Lilliana said as she turned to wrap her arms around her father. "You deserve more hugs than I could ever give you, Daddy."

Her father squeezed her tightly in his embrace. Nothing compared to a hug from her father. It made her feel safe and loved. She meant what she told him. She could never give or receive enough hugs from him.

"Okay princess, I have work to do and some things to discuss with your mother. Go get packing or you'll never be ready to leave on time."

"I love you two, you really are the best parents, and you are right, I have a lot to do. Gemma is coming for tea soon as well."

Lilliana left the room with a huge smile on her face. The talk had gone a lot better than she hoped. Gemma would arrive any minute and she needed to pack. She doubted sleep would be easy tonight with all the excitement. As she entered the hall she heard the front door open and Gemma stepped inside. Gemma looked over at her and strolled to her side.

"Oh good, you're here," she said as she walked over to give her friend a hug. "Although I've already ordered tea and scones. Let's go into the sitting room and talk."

Gemma followed Lilliana into the sitting room, removed her pelisse and set it on a chair, and then sat on the settee. She turned and gave her full attention to her best friend.

"So what's the urgency?" she asked.

"He's leaving tomorrow. I need you to have the carriage bring me to the ship in the morning," Lilliana explained. "Everything will have to be stepped up a day. Can you manage it?"

"Of course," Gemma agreed. "It's a small thing to arrange to have one of our carriages pick you up in the morning. Are you sure you want to do this? I have to ask one final time."

"Yes, I do. I told you how much I needed to leave."

"I know, but Mr. Collins isn't exactly what I expected you to sail away with. He's a very handsome man. I don't want you to do anything you might regret later."

"Nonsense. I can handle Mr. Collins, besides I don't plan on getting married. Maybe a little fling is something I should consider."

"What?" Gemma's sanguine curls fell over her face as her emerald eyes widened in shock.

"Why shouldn't I know what passion is like? I don't need to save my virtue for my future husband if I don't plan on having one," Lilliana explained.

"There can be other ramifications of finding out what passion is besides losing your virtue, Lily."

"I'm aware of that. I didn't say I decided to experience yet, I'm only considering it. I need to make sure I'm okay with the possible complications first."

"Good, at least you are stopping to think about it first. I don't want you to make a mistake."

"I don't believe in mistakes. Everything we do is a life lesson. It is through those so-called mistakes that we learn and grow. If I decide to give myself to Mr. Collins, it will be a wonderful thing. I refuse to think of it as a possible error in judgment."

"I know you are going to do whatever you choose to do. I just hope that it's the right decision for your continued happiness. I only want what is best for you."

"I know you do." Lilliana acknowledged. "I'm truly going to miss you."

"I know, but you need to do this." Gemma's eyes held a hint of sadness in them as she gazed at her.

They turned when a maid brought in a tray with

the tea and scones Lilliana had ordered. She carried the tray over to them and placed it on a table beside them.

"Do you need me to pour miss?" the maid asked.

"No, I can handle it. Thank you, Melly."

Melly curtsied and walked out of the room. Lilliana turned toward the tea and poured some into two cups and handed one to Gemma.

"Now that the details are settled, let's talk about a lighter subject." Lilliana said.

"What did you have in mind?"

"Oh, I don't know anything. What do you think of this weather we are having? Scorching hot one day and cold and rainy the next"

"That's England for you." Gemma said with a laugh.

The mood lightened and Lilliana sat back on the settee. She needed to enjoy one last afternoon with Gemma before she no longer could. She needed the memory to take with her and hold tight. As much as she needed to leave, it also occurred to her that she'd be entirely alone in her new home. If she could take Gemma with her, she would have included it in her scheme. It's too bad it couldn't be done, because Gemma's friendship held a special place in her heart.

CHAPTER SIX

*A*fter Rand had time to think about this foolhardy plan he realized the sooner he left the better. He trusted Lilliana to have all the details set, but he didn't hold a lot of conviction that her father would not get wind his daughter's plans. If it had any chance of working they needed to leave with all due haste. So after he left the ball he went to his ship and ordered the preparations to set sail. After that he only had one problem left, he had a whole day to kill and no idea what to do with himself.

The day had been excruciating for him. He found himself pacing the length of the ship most of the day in anticipation of her arrival. Sleep failed to arrive that night and made him cranky while he waited for the sun to rise. In his note he told her to arrive to set sail after the sun had risen in the sky. It made him happy to realize she knew the importance of punctuality as he watched the Earl of Devon's carriage arrive at the docks. As she stepped out of the carriage, she raised her hands block out the sun as she got a look at his ship. Rand turned and motioned two deck hands to follow him as he wandered down the gangplank to greet her.

"A couple crew members are going to load your trunks on the ship," he told her. "We set sail in less than an hour."

"Good. I don't want to wait to set sail. I'm glad we are leaving immediately."

"If you follow me I'll show you where you'll be staying during the voyage."

Lilliana followed him onto the ship and below deck to the cabin she'd be residing in the length of the journey to South Carolina. The cabin was small, but he hoped she'd make do with the sparse conditions. Especially, since it happened to be the only cabin available for her use. He watched her walk into the room and take off her pelisse. She set it on the table and turned toward him.

"Thank you for allowing me to sail with you, Mr. Collins."

"Please call me, Rand."

"I'm not sure that's wise. It's entirely too informal," Lilliana responded.

"My ship's a rather informal venue." With a smile he continued, "Trust me, it's easier if you acquiesce to my request."

He watched as she mulled over his words. Rand hoped she gave in and called him by his given name. He ached to hear his name pass through her lips. Little informalities had to start somewhere. Giving her permission to use his given name helped to ease her slowly into his strategy of lulling her to his will. He had a plan of his own and he intended to succeed.

"All right," she said with a sigh. "If you insist, I will call you Rand. I still think it's a bad idea though."

"Duly noted, but I'm glad you are willing to give it a try regardless."

"I suppose if I'm to call you Rand, you must call me Lily. Only my closest friends and family do."

"I'm honored to be amongst that small circle of people. If you'll excuse me, I have much to do before we depart," Rand replied.

"Rand wait; I have one question before you leave."

He turned back when he heard his name; a shudder rolled over him at the sound. The more she said it the easier it appeared to come out of her mouth. He loved hearing it and hoped to hear her say it for the rest of his life. It breathed life into him where none had previously existed.

"What do you need to know?"

"It's about the bargain we made."

He could see the hesitation in her words. Clearly she had been thinking about the payment that they agreed upon. Good, he wanted her to think about him kissing her and often, because he intended to do it more than she knew or expected him to.

"You mean the kiss you agreed to let me have," he responded.

"Yes. See I had more time to think about it..."

"I hope you are not going to go back on our bargain. It's not too late for you to go home."

"I have no intention of going back on our bargain. I'd like to modify it slightly, if you are willing."

"Okay, you have piqued my interest. How would you like to change our deal?" Rand asked.

"I make no excuses for my innocence. My upbringing demanded no less. What I'd like to do is rectify that with your help."

Surprised, he responded, "Are you asking me to take your innocence?" That couldn't be right, and yet he felt every inch of his body preparing to teach her everything she wanted to know. He hoped to God that she meant it because he wanted to be the only one she'd ever know. Lilliana belonged to him and in time she would realize it.

"I'm not sure exactly what I am asking of you. I just get this feeling when I'm close to you. I don't ever plan on getting married so..." her words trailed off. She started to pace in the small room her anxiety starting to show.

"You figure I'm as good as anyone in showing you what passion is all about," he finished for her.

Rand's stomach dropped as her words sank in. The pain, a sucker punch, he hadn't been expecting. At first he had no idea how to respond to her because her words were still floating through his brain. Never marry? He would work on changing her mind. As much as he wanted to teach her everything she desired. Rand knew if he did she'd never consider being his wife. There would be no reason to. She'd get all she wanted out of him and toss him aside in time. That didn't mean he couldn't seduce her to his way of thinking without actually sealing the deal.

"Yes," she said nodding in his direction. "I know its risqué, but I feel I can trust you."

"You shouldn't trust me Lily."

She stopped and stared at him as if she actually saw him for the first time. Her gaze rolled over him starting at his feet and resting at his eyes. With the intake of her breath he knew she saw the strength of desire in his eyes. She just didn't know the full extent of what he wanted to do with and to her. She'd find out one day, but not as soon as she liked.

"Regardless I do. Please consider what I'm asking."

"No."

"Why not?"

"Because you don't know what you are asking of me. I don't heel to commands," he countered.

"I don't understand. What do you want from me?"

"It's simple enough Lily." He crossed the short distance of the room, pulled her into his arms, and whispered in her ear. "I want everything."

"Then give me what I want." Lilliana's face was flushed, and her breaths came out in short pants.

"No. Things will go at a pace I set. I will not give into your demands."

"Why must you be so obstinate? You want me. Take what I'm offering you," she pleaded.

"Maybe I will, maybe I won't. In the meantime, I will take the kiss you owe me."

Rand tilted her head and leaned down capturing her lips with his. A small sound of surprise came out of her mouth, and he took advantage of its opening. He touched her tongue with his, and she innocently followed his lead. Their tongues intertwined as he gently glided his over hers. His lips caressed hers as he learned her taste. Her hands wound around his neck and her fingers ran with abandon through his hair. Rand lifted his lips and trailed them over her cheeks and chin in light kisses. He drew back and looked at her half closed eyes. When they fluttered open, he saw a hazy desire filling the blue depths, a need matching his. He placed a quick kiss on her forehead before he let her go. If he didn't put some distance between them, he wouldn't be able to stop. He would need to move slowly, if he intended to win her forever.

"That's enough for now. I must go." With a half-smile on his face he said, "Think of me while I'm gone." He turned and left before she could answer him.

That had gone a lot better than he planned. He didn't have any doubts about winning her. When he wanted something bad enough, Rand never lost. Winning Lilliana would be an enormous battle, and he hoped her own nature would work against her belief that marriage didn't work for her. In the meantime, he had a ship to get ready to sail and no time to lose. He marched up on deck to get going before he lost something he treasured more than his own life. Lilliana Marsden now belonged to him. Damn anyone if they tried to take her away from him.

As he reached the top of the deck he saw Lilliana trunks ready to be taken below deck at a later time. Rand walked to the stern of the ship and located his bosun and first mate.

"Is the ship ready to set sail?"

"Yes, Captain," his bosun answered. "Sal and Jim are going to take the lady's trunks to her cabin. Do you want us to lift the anchor now?"

"Yes. It's time to go home," he told them. "The sooner we get there to better. Give the order."

"Aye, Aye Captain" the bosun said and left to follow Rand's orders.

"Do you need us to do anything else before we leave Captain?" the first mate asked.

"No, we don't have any cargo this trip. Just make sure the navigation goes well. We have a good wind and should be out to sea soon. I'll be in my cabin if you need me. You're in charge for the time being."

Rand walked back below deck to his cabin. He

passed the closed door of Lily's cabin and for a brief moment considered knocking on it and kissing her senseless again. Deciding against it he continued on to his cabin. No reason to rock the boat just yet. A good seduction took time.

CHAPTER SEVEN

*S*everal hours later, Lilliana stood in the middle of her cabin and crossed her arms over her chest. A mere kiss left her with feelings she never experienced before with anyone else. Rand told her to think about him, and she thought about nothing else. Phantom tingles grazed across the tops of her lips and she could almost feel the slight pressure of Rand's as they caressed her. She ran her fingers across her lips, trying to understand the emotions swirling inside of her. In her first season, she had allowed one of her many beaus to kiss her. It hadn't stirred any emotions within her, and so she tossed it aside as something she didn't really care to experience again. Perhaps she had dismissed kissing too soon. Rand clearly knew what he was doing, and Lilliana realized with the right person doing the kissing it could be quite enjoyable. It now held an appeal it never had before.

Rand generated the most wonderful feelings, and she wanted to find out where they all would lead. Perhaps he had been right in denying her idea of a more clandestine affair right away. A challenge just made things a bit more interesting. After his kiss, Lilliana knew she wanted to explore all of her options, and she intended to get her way. Plans could be adjusted to reflect necessary changes.

Marriage and forever had never been on her agenda. That desire hadn't really changed, but she had a small thought that perhaps she wouldn't mind having Rand around long term. She now desired him in a way she hadn't needed anyone else. Lilliana started to scheme in her head how to make him hers. Her life would be exceedingly different with him by her side. Perhaps she could talk him into living with her permanently without the benefit of marriage.

Her ideals adapted to include him in every part of her life. Rand could help her run the plantation in South Carolina. So far he appeared to be a good man, when he hadn't jumped at her offer she learned what she needed to know about the depth of his character. He told her not to trust him, but clearly she could. The man hadn't wanted to take advantage of her and refused to take her innocence. She just needed to find a way to get him around to her way of thinking.

A knock on the door brought her out of her thoughts. She strolled to the door and opened it. She found Rand leaning against the doorframe with a cocky smile on his face.

"Did you miss me?"

He wore an overconfident smile on his handsome chiseled face. His brown hair looked a bit ruffled from working topside of the ship. It caused Lily to want to run her fingers through his hair and feel it for herself. He stood before her as if expecting her to give into the whims crossing through her mind. Cocky bastard believed he had won her over already. Okay he had, but he didn't need to know that just yet. If they had a chance, some boundaries had to be set up and established in advance. She garnered that much watching her parents over the years. Her father knew exactly how far he could push her mother before her she exploded with temper.

"Not at all." Lilliana brushed him aside. "I've been too busy to give you a second thought. Are you here for a reason?"

"Busy really? Doing what exactly?" he inquired.

"I started writing some correspondence I'll need to mail once I arrive in South Carolina. I'm going to have to let my parents know where I am eventually. I didn't dare leave anything at home to make them aware of my intentions."

"Probably a wise decision on your part. How will you explain to them your decision to leave?" Rand asked.

"I'll tell them the truth. They know I've wanted to live on the plantation for over a year now. I loved it when we visited as a child. I grew up in England, but South Carolina calls to my soul."

"Then why all the subterfuge?" Rand raised his eyebrow questionably.

Lilliana raised her left eyebrow at his question. "I don't know what you mean."

"You know exactly what I mean. If you love the property as much as you say why deny you the opportunity to visit. What are you not telling me?"

"Ah I see your point. Technically I'm not supposed to visit without one of my parents with me. I didn't want to give them a chance to deny me the opportunity to go. I have the better part of a year until I'm old enough to gain the majority to go on my own. Father didn't want to let his only daughter go off to another country just yet. He was adamant about my staying home as long as possible. We had many arguments about the issue."

"I can't say I blame him. If I had a daughter I'd probably be a bit overprotective myself."

Lilliana shrugged her shoulders and turned away from him. "Yes, well there's overprotective and then there's smothering. Father tends to lean towards the latter."

"Most fathers are," he said. "At least the good ones."

Lilliana turned back around and face him. "Probably, I just know how my father is. I love him, but he can be a bit...relentless at times. Probably stems from his pirating days."

"Wait, what did you say?" Rand asked with a stunned expression on his face.

"Oh, I must have forgotten to mention that to you. My father used to sail his ship the *Sea Rover* as Pirate Thor Williams. It's how my parents met."

"But he's a viscount." Rand's bafflement at her pronouncement was evident in his words.

"And he used to be a pirate. What's your point?"

"That it just doesn't make sense. How can a member of the English aristocracy have been a pirate?" He raised his hands showcasing his frustration.

"I'm not sure on the details." Lilliana shrugged. "They are a bit sketchy. It had something to do with my mother's grandpere and attempted murder. Suffice to say he had a long road back to claiming his title."

Rand began to rub his temples. Lilliana knew she had to tell him about her father's past. The possibility of him getting his own ship ready and coming after them remained high in her concerns. As far as she knew a faster ship than the *Sea Rover* didn't exist. Her father had been excited to make the necessary modifications to make the ship faster than in his pirate days. She hoped they had a good head start before he realized she'd boarded a ship headed to America.

"You are going to be the death of me," he exclaimed. "How long do we have?"

"I don't know what you mean?" Lilliana faked innocence at his remark.

"I mean how long before your ex-pirate father comes after you?"

"Um, well, I'm not sure. I guess it depends on how long it takes him to realize I am not spending the week at the country estate of the Earl of Devon."

"I give it a day tops before he is getting his ship ready to set sail after us."

"I'm afraid you may be right," she agreed. "At some point they will see Gemma out in society and question my whereabouts. The only good news is that it'll take a while to get the *Sea Rover* ready to set sail. I happen to have overheard him say he planned to careen his ship. The rest of the fleet owned by Marsden Shipping is elsewhere earning their keep. We may have a while before he has access to a ship capable of coming after us."

"Really? How advantageous for you. No wonder you wanted to get on a ship heading for America as soon as possible," Rand retorted.

"I told you I had a plan."

"Indeed you did I just didn't realize how extensive the details were."

"I have always believed the details are what made the best schemes possible," Lilliana said. "I'm good at plotting and planning."

"I noticed," Rand said with a half-smile.

"You're not mad at me are you?" Lilliana leaned

into him and attempted to cajole him into a more relaxed state.

Rand raised his eyebrow at her questioning her methods, but allowed her to lean her body farther into his. "Not at all, dear. I may have to readjust our course, but I think I can manage to evade your pirate father."

"He isn't a pirate anymore."

"My apologies, your *former* pirate father."

With a petulant smile she said, "You should apologize. He's reformed, mostly."

"Lilliana, dear I'll say one thing about you, things are never dull with you around."

So far things were going as planned. She adjusted the details to include winning over Rand, and he currently fell in line with each one. When she decided she needed him in her life, she realized she'd have to tell him all the family's dirty secrets. He'd taken the fact her father had been a pirate rather well in her estimation. Now to step up her plan to get what she wanted. She got a little taste of desire and craved more. She began to rub her hands across his broad chest and massaged her fingertips into his well-toned muscles. When she noticed his breathing change, she looked up into his eyes to get his full attention.

"Did you stop by for any particular reason?" she asked coyly.

He leaned down and his mouth grazed her ear. Lilliana shivered as his breath caressed her neck. He whispered, "I have many reasons for stopping in to see you."

"Name one," she replied.

"I'd like to kiss you again."

"What's stopping you?" Lilliana had trouble breathing. The pace of her heart quickened, and she became heated from being near him.

"The fact that you want it as much as I do." Rand took a step back. "I believe you are a closet wanton."

"I believe you just insulted me," Lilliana retorted.

"I would never do any such thing. I adore you. However, you are in a hurry to lose your innocence. I'm not sure you realize what you are ready to throw away. I'm trying to be a gentleman."

"Nonsense, I know exactly what I'm offering you. I never asked you to play the part of gentleman. Why not just give in? You want me as much as I want you."

"Your pirate father for one. If he catches up to us I'd like to say I left you unspoiled. It could very well preserve my life." Rand folded his hands over his chest as he looked at her.

"I don't believe you. My father has nothing to do with your intentions towards me."

"Maybe you're right, but what if you're wrong? Nevertheless, when or if I decide to make love to you it will be my decision. You've already given me consent to try. I'd rather it be at a moment of my choosing."

"I think you are being unreasonable." Lilliana pushed her bottom lip out into a pout at his refusal to give in to her demands.

"And I think you are acting like a spoiled brat."

Spoiled brat? How dare he? *That man doesn't know a lick about me and he referred to me as a brat and a wanton. Maybe I should just give him exactly what he believes me to be.* She stalked over to him and threw her arms around him, pulling his head down. Her lips crushed his breathing life into her frustrations. With each movement the constant turmoil of her emotions bled into the kiss, their tongues dueling for control. Lilliana pulled her tongue back in her mouth and bit down on his bottom lip. She kissed away the soreness with a gentle sweep of her lips to soothe the ache she created. Rand pulled her into his embrace, and her hands roamed through his hair to bring his head closer to hers. Rand groaned and put his arms around her so he could deepen the kiss. Finally, he was acting in a way that would lead to what she desired from him. After what seemed an eternity, Rand wrenched himself away from her and put some distance between them.

"Damn you woman. You drive me insane."

"Thank you, I do try." An impish smile formed on her face as desire flowed through her.

He laughed and continued to back away from her. It made her feel powerful to know the kiss had rattled him to the core. Yes, she believed that every one of her plans progressed nicely.

"I think I may have taken on more than I can handle," he said.

"Oh, you don't think you can handle little ol' me?"

"Not tonight imp. I only came down to invite you to dinner. You distracted me from my original purpose."

"Backing away in defeat then?"

"You can win this little skirmish love." He smiled. "But I promise you, I'll win the war."

"I guess we'll see about that." She gave him a searing look as she said, "I've never lost before and I don't intend to now."

"Well then its time you learned how to take defeat with graciousness."

"Grace is my middle name." She gave him a devilish smile. "I personify it."

"Touché my dear," he said. "I'll give you that much. Let's agree to disagree at this point. I need to eat, I'm famished."

"So am I, but not for food," she replied.

He groaned as he turned around and started to walk out of the cabin. After he crossed the threshold, he turned back around and looked at her. Her words had the desired outcome; Rand appeared to be struggling to get his emotions under control.

"If you decide you're hungry for real food, come up to the galley. I'm heading there now. Perhaps I'll see you later."

"Only if you choose to visit me in my cabin again." She threw the words at him to see what kind of reaction she could continue to garner from him. Battling with words was something she did rather well.

"I bid you goodnight," he said and walked away.

That little encounter had definitely gone in her favor, although he left a bit quicker than she would have liked. He called their battle of wills a war. When she told him she didn't intend to lose she meant it. If he wanted a war then he had one and he better be prepared for anything. In her limited experience she knew that everything happened to be fair involving desire and war. This confrontation of his included both and she planned on using everything in her arsenal to triumph. Lilliana liked nothing better than winning; after all she happened to be good at it.

CHAPTER EIGHT

*R*and walked along the deck and took a deep breath. The more time he spent in the lovely imp's company the more power he lost over the situation. Stopping by to invite her to dinner a week ago had been a strain on his control. He needed to rein things in a bit. Never in his wildest dreams did he imagine a woman like her existed. Lilliana Marsden's reckless behavior stirred his own. The trip back home would be his undoing. He didn't believe he could resist the entire three weeks it would take to reach port. In order to keep his hands off of her he had done everything to avoid her. Retreat did not look good on him. Taking a step back made it possible for him to look at things with more clarity. He now had a plan of action and he intended to implement it soon.

"Have you been avoiding me?"

Rand could almost feel Lilliana standing behind him. He leaned on the ship railing to look out at the turquoise waves as they rolled across the ocean. He figured out she didn't really like being ignored and deliberately pretended he hadn't heard her. Keeping his gaze forward, he waited for her to explode.

"Damn you, answer me." The palm of her hand met his back with a resounding *thud*, leaving a trail of sharp tingles in its place.

He turned his head and looked over his shoulder. His gaze traveled over her from top to bottom. He noticed that she had not donned a gown, but instead put on breeches and a tunic draped in a cuffed red jacket. He had to stop himself from growling in approval. In the sunlight, he could see the outline of her breasts beneath the white blouse. The breeches fit her perfectly, and he got a good view of her legs and hips. He ached to ask her to spin for him so he could also see how they fit her derriere. Instead he kept to his plan of indifference and acted like her presence didn't matter to him.

"Can I help you?" he asked.

"Yes, you can give me your attention."

"I didn't realize that attending to you had been made a requirement of allowing you to travel aboard my ship. I apologize if I am slacking in my duties," he said with a droll smile.

"Don't be absurd. I never demanded that you give me all of your attention. But I'm bored and I hoped you might want to spend some time with me." Her bottom lip lifted into a pout as she folder her arms across her pert breasts.

"I'm kind of busy right now. I doubt I'll be able to spend any time with you."

"Doing what? Ascertaining if the ocean might dry up this century?" Sarcasm dripped from every word.

"No need to get testy with me, dear," he said absentmindedly. "I am just taking a small break to enjoy the view. I love how the sun looks as it rises on the horizon."

"So what do you have to do that is taking all of your time?" she demanded.

"Oh little things, you know like sailing this ship. I'm to take over from the first mate in a few minutes," he explained. "Unless you'd rather I leave it to fate and let the ship roam wherever it wants to."

He couldn't help needling her. Her face flushed, and her eyes became a stormy blue; she was lovelier when anger overtook her features. He liked it almost as much as when her face glowed with passion. If he couldn't see his favorite expression on her face, he'd take the look of rage instead. At least it mirrored desire a little bit.

"Don't be ridiculous," she retorted. "I understand the necessity of steering the ship. I just didn't realize that you actually had a part in it."

Rand shrugged his shoulders at her response. "Well, I am the captain of the ship. It stands to reason I'd have something to do with how it is run."

"Oh, I thought you just owned the ship. You actually captain it as well?"

"I do on this one. The other ships in my line have captains I've hired to work with my company."

She walked past him to lean on the railing, stopping to look out at the wide expanse of the ocean. Rand got a chance to look at her from behind. He knew that he'd enjoy that particular view while she wore trousers, and the vision before Rand did not disappoint him. His hands itched to touch her, so he took a step back before he gave in to temptation. She turned around and looked up at him.

"So you leave often to sail your own ship?" she asked.

"I don't stay home that often. I haven't had a reason to," he replied.

"Do you even have a home of your own?"

"No, not really. I stay at a boarding house when I find myself in South Carolina. I didn't see the point of building a home when I'm rarely there. I make my living by sailing. I usually stick around long enough to do some accounting and once it's completed I order the ship ready to go out again."

"It sounds like a lonely existence," she said.

"I didn't notice it. I kept busy and I made money. It's all that mattered to me."

"You don't want a family of your own?"

"No. I didn't think I'd make a good husband. So I believed I made the right choice in devoting my life to building my shipping company," he responded.

"I don't believe you."

"What is there to doubt?" he asked. "My inability to make some woman happy or that I enjoyed my so called lonely existence?"

She stared at him as if trying to dissect his meaning. How could he explain to her that until he met her nothing else mattered? He found purpose in building his business. He had no family and no one that depended on him. That only left one thing for him to do with his life. He had plenty of ambition to spare, and he focused all of his energy creating something for him to believe in.

"I doubt both. I know you are capable of making a woman happy if you set your mind to it. No one enjoys a lonely existence. Why have you punished yourself with the belief you are better off alone?"

"I have no family. I don't know what it's like to be surrounded by people that love you. I'm not punishing myself. I'm living the only way I know how," Rand explained.

"How long have you been alone, Rand?"

"All my life. I never knew my parents. I grew up in an orphanage. I ran away when I turned ten and got a job on the first sailing vessel that would hire me. They told me my mother died giving birth to me and no one knew who my father could be. My mother named me before she took her last breath. No one could afford to keep me so they dropped me off at the nearest church. That is how I ended up in a home for boys."

"Have you ever considered finding your father?" she asked.

"No. I don't even know where to look. The only thing I have to go on is my mother's name. That doesn't exactly tell me who my father might have been."

"If you don't mind me asking, what is her name?"

"Emily Collins," he told her. "But as I said it doesn't help trace down my wayward father."

"I'm sorry," Lilliana replied. "I didn't mean to bring up something so sad. I'm glad you told me though. It explains why you are so comfortable being alone."

"You have no reason to be sorry, Lily. It is what it is. I don't have a problem talking about it. You are incredibly lucky to have parents who love you. Remember that when they come after you because you know they will."

"I do know it. No matter how much I don't want them to, they will. I know they worry about me. I only hope that once they see me they will let me stay," she said with resignation in her voice.

"Good. It will be easier if you realize that," he muttered. "I will leave you with that to think about. I need to relieve the first mate now."

"Can I come with you?" she asked. "I promise I won't bother you. Well at least too much. I'm just tired of my own company and you are the only person I know on this ship."

He thought about what her company would be like as he stood at the helm of his ship. Once the picture formed in his mind he couldn't let it go. He couldn't avoid her forever if he hoped to get her to want to stay with him. He figured he could fight his desire for her if he had something to keep his hands busy. There would be no harm in allowing her to keep him company as he kept the ship on course. His hands would remain damn near tied to the helm allowing him to refrain from giving into his baser instincts.

"Yeah," he murmured. "I don't mind if you keep me company. Follow me."

He turned away from her and began to stroll toward the wheel that steered the ship. As he approached, he saw the first mate keeping it steady and on course. He didn't know for sure if Lilliana followed him, but he figured she must have considering she asked to keep him company.

"I'm here to relieve you. Go get some sleep so you can take over later on this evening," he told his first mate.

"Aye, Aye Captain. I'm mighty tired. I'll see you later. Good day miss."

Rand turned and watched as the first mate bowed his head to Lilliana. She returned the gesture before joining him at the helm. She sat down on the deck, crossed the legs, and rested her back on the mast near the helm. Her hands rested on the deck as she leaned back to look at the sky.

"What is running through your mind?" he asked her.

"Have you ever looked at clouds and thought they reminded you of something?"

"No, I can't say I have."

"My brother and I used to play this game as children. We would lie down on the ground and watch as the big fluffy clouds floated by us. Sometimes they reminded of us of things in our lives: a bunny, a flower, or even a horse drawn carriage. It became one of our favorite games. When I looked up at the sky I remembered what a great childhood I had."

"Are you feeling a little homesick?"

"No not at all. I just wished you had even an ounce of what I had growing up. I had two adoring parents and you didn't even have one."

"I told you not to feel sorry for me, Lily. I'm content with how my life turned out."

"That doesn't mean that you shouldn't strive for more from life, Rand. You deserve everything, happiness included. You're a good man and you should have a little joy," she told him.

"I promise you I will," he said with a cocky smile. "It's just a work in progress."

"Good," she said with an impish smile. "In the

meantime, I'll do my part in ensuring you continue to work on it."

He laughed and turned his attention back to keeping the ship on course. They sat in silence for an hour before she got up and stretched her legs. She walked over to him, wrapped her arms around his waist, and rested her head on his back. Rand enjoyed the feel of her arms wound around him. He could almost hear his heart drumming in his ears as it began to beat faster. He closed his eyes and absorbed the feeling. If he could he would turn around and hug her close to him, but he had to keep his attention on the helm of the ship.

In that moment he knew he loved her, because with her arms enveloping he let himself feel for the first time in his life. Rand had been alone his whole life. He didn't depend on anyone and didn't look to anyone else to fulfill any of his needs. Lilliana made him want things he never knew he wanted. With her he could feel himself lighten inside. He thought he didn't want anyone in his life until her. That need had been buried deep inside of him a long time ago.

"As fun as this has been I'm kind of tired. I'm going to go lay down in my cabin. If you want me you know where to find me," she told him.

Rand nodded in agreement. "That I do."

He watched for a moment as she traipsed across the deck. Enjoying the view of her derriere in breeches one last time, he hoped she continued to dress in a similar fashion the rest of the voyage. He let out a small breath of relief once he could no longer see her. He had managed to keep his hands to himself and have a pleasant conversation with her. He only had to make it another two weeks and get her safely tucked away at her family plantation.

CHAPTER NINE

*L*ily walked out of her cabin and up to the deck. Rand hadn't openly admitted to it but she knew that he had been avoiding her. Once she tracked him down he at least allowed her to keep him company. She hoped to further her agenda and get him to see how an affair would benefit them both. To be honest, she wanted more than an affair—she wanted him to be her lover for life. Marriage still seemed too risky of an endeavor for her, but the more time she spent with Rand the more she knew she needed him in her life. Her plans now included him at her side. She just had to find a way to make that happen.

She roamed aimlessly along the deck and stared out into the ocean pondering what the next step in her plan should be. Seduction could hold the key to achieving her goal. Perhaps it was time to discover where the captain slept. She could ambush him in his cabin and let things take their natural course. Rand had said if he wanted her he would do it at a time of his choosing, but so far that time had not taken place. Lilliana was beginning to get restless waiting for him to make a move. She did not do well sitting idly by waiting for something to happen. Her nature leaned more towards taking action and seeing what happened afterward.

Not watching where her feet took her she ran into a deck hand and fell back on her derriere. She braced herself with her hands and looked up into a pair of brown eyes and a concerned frown.

"I'm sorry miss. I didn't mean to knock you down," he apologized.

"No it's not your fault..." She realized she didn't know his name. She stared at him a bit bewildered; Lilliana hadn't bothered to get to know anyone on board the ship. It gave her an idea on what to do to not only gain Rand's attention, but also help to alleviate some of her boredom.

"Sal," the deck hand told her.

"What?" Did he just say something about sailing?

"My name is Sal, miss."

"Oh. I feel silly now. I thought you were talking about the sails."

"I never thought about that actually. Sal is just a nickname."

"Really? What's your actual name?"

"Salvatorio," he said with a grimace. "It's a bit long, but it's a family name."

"I kind of like it." She smiled. "Sal perhaps you can help me with something."

"I will if I can, but first let me help you up."

He held out his hand and Lilliana gave him hers. Sal helped pull her up so she stood beside him.

"Thank you."

"You're welcome. What can I help you with?" he asked.

"I'm going a bit stir crazy. Do you happen to play any card games?"

"I'm fairly good at whist. I could get a couple of other men to play a game with you. A few of us have some free time right now," Sal replied.

"Oh splendid. I just need to retrieve my cards from my trunk. Where would you like to meet?"

"We can meet in the galley. We have a couple hours before the next meal. After that we are back on duty."

"Good. I shall see you soon then." Lilliana nodded and walked off.

When she reached her cabin she dug through the trunk for her cards. She didn't think Rand would like the idea of her playing cards and entertaining some of the crew. The only thing she had uncertainty about was how to get him to realize she was embroiled in a game of whist with some of his deck hands. She hoped that he would just stumble upon them, and she could get both of her agendas accomplished. Locating the cards, she put them in the pocket of her trousers and skipped up toward meet them in the galley. She sashayed as she made her way to the galley with a huge smile on her face. When she entered the room she saw three men sitting at the table. Sal she knew from her little accident on the deck.

"Good you are all here. Introduce me to your friends, Sal," she demanded.

"This guy here with the hook nose is Jimmy and the scary looking one is Georgie." Sal introduced her to his two shipmates.

She raised her eyebrows at him. "Scary?"

"I'm harmless, I can't help how big I am," Georgie explained.

"All right then. Let's get started. I'll cut the cards

first to see who we partner up with." Lilliana began to shuffle the cards as she spoke. She cut the cars and drew a seven. The men followed suit and cut the deck to reveal a card. Sal drew an eight, Georgie a jack, and Jimmy a king.

"It looks like I'm partners with Sal. Do you mind if I deal first?" Lilliana asked.

"No, I don't see any reason why not." Georgie replied. The other two murmured their consent as well.

Lilliana sat down and began to shuffle the cards with dexterous hands. She placed them to her left to let Georgie cut them. She picked them back up and started to deal thirteen cards face down to each of them. After dealing all the cards, she flipped the top one over to reveal the trump.

"Hearts are trump gentlemen. Let's begin." She told them.

With a laugh they grabbed their cards and began to play in earnest. They played a grueling game for an hour before Rand found them. Sal and Lilliana were ahead, but barely. She was so engrossed in the game she hadn't realized he had walked in until he spoke.

"What are you up to?" Rand demanded.

She looked up into his eyes and smiled. "I think that's fairly obvious. We are playing Whist."

"Not a good idea. Time to break this game up. Sal, Jimmy, Georgie go see the bosun and report for duty."

"But we have an hour until..." Sal began to say.

Rand interrupted, "Don't argue. If you want to keep your position once we reach port you will follow my orders."

The three of them got up and walked away grumbling as they left the room.

"Was that necessary? We were having fun." Lilliana's voice filled with anger.

"Yes. I don't believe these men will over step any boundaries, but I happen to know that you want to lose that innocence of yours. I won't have you tempting them into doing something to jeopardize their livelihoods."

"Don't be ridiculous. I had no intention of propositioning any of them. I do have standards."

"Do you? You damn near accosted me the first day on the ship. How am I to know exactly what you will or will not do?"

"That's not fair. You are the only man I have ever asked that. I truly believed you would make a wonderful lover. Apparently I need to once again readjust my views. Clearly I was mistaken on your worthiness."

"Oh, so now I'm not good enough?" he asked. "Does that mean you are going to find another one of the men and ask them help you lose your innocence?"

Rand's face began to get red with each word he enunciated. His eyes shot daggers in her direction as he folded his arms across his chest.

"Maybe I should. You don't want me so what difference does it make who I give myself to?" Lilliana glared at him.

"I never said I didn't want you."

"Well, you sure fooled me. You keep avoiding me and definitely turn down every offer I make to you. You win, I give up."

Lilliana got up to storm away, but Rand grabbed her hand and spun her into his arms. She tilted her head to look up into his eyes. The lines of his mouth were tight as he pressed them together and stared at her.

"You can't give up. I won't allow it."

"It's not up to you to allow anything, Rand. You have no right to dictate to me."

He ignored her word and with tenderness lowered his lips to hers. This kiss was different as he coaxed her into yielding to him. Slow and gentle he caressed her in such a way her anger evaporated. A different kind of passion took its place. Heat spread through her and the kiss took on another level. It didn't take long before she ran her hands through his hair and pulled him closer to her. The kiss overtook them as they battled for control. Determined to win, Lilliana took a different strategy. In this war between them he had stepped back and took control of the situation. He always had the upper hand. That needed to change if she wanted to win. So as much as she enjoyed the kiss she knew it needed to end. In order for her to get him where she wanted him he needed to chase her. This game needed to change, and she knew how to make that happen. She pulled away from him and took a step away to gain some distance.

"You don't get to do that whenever you want, Rand. I rescind my offer. I don't want to be your lover anymore." She licked her lips. "The kisses have been enjoyable, but this just isn't working for me. Maybe you're right; I need to look into finding someone else to introduce me to the art of love making."

She saw the dumbstruck look on his face before she turned and walked away. Maybe now things would go her way. She hoped she didn't miscalculate in her scheme and he didn't do the opposite; her intention was to present him with a challenge. All she could do now was sit back and wait to see if he took the bait.

CHAPTER TEN

*R*and stood there and watched Lily walk away. Her beautiful derriere displayed nicely in her trousers. He wanted to cup her ass in his hands and pull her back into his arms. The more he saw her wearing men's attire the more he desired her. *Who am I kidding? I will want her no matter what she is wearing.* Damned if he didn't understand what the hell just happened between them? That kiss amped up things, and he wanted to strip all of her clothes off and just give in to her demands. He should be glad she halted things when she did, but all it did was leave him confused. No way in hell was he going to allow her to find another lover. If he had to give in to her demands first and convince her around to marriage he would. That plan didn't sit too well with him though. He wanted her to believe marriage between them was a good thing. Passion could be fleeting, and he wanted more than that with her. He needed her to love him as much as he had grown to love her.

He scrubbed his hands over his face and weighed his options. Perhaps avoiding her wasn't the best idea. Clearly she didn't want him to keep his hands off of her so he would just give her want she wanted. Short of the actual act that is, he still believed it was best to wait before making love to her. He believed they could be happy together and wanted Lilliana to be his wife. The best way to start changing her mind was to give her a little taste of what that future could hold. Once she started to crave him and what he could do for her it wouldn't take much for the rest of it to follow. With that idea in his head he decided to pay her a visit in her cabin. *Don't want me anymore? Well we will just see about that.*

Rand sauntered out of the galley and down to Lilliana's cabin. He rapped lightly on her door and waited for her to open it. When she did he couldn't help the slight intake of breath at the sight of her. Her hair was floating down her back in endless black waves. She still wore her trousers and tunic. Her blue eyes shined as she looked up at him.

"What do you want Rand? I thought we settled everything."

"You may have, but I'm not nearly done with you."

"Well that's a shame because as far as I'm concerned there isn't anything else between us. You can leave now."

She started to shut the door, but he stopped it with his hand. He pushed the door open and strode inside of her cabin. He shut the door with a quiet click behind him and turned the lock.

"What are you doing?" Lilliana asked.

"I believe we have a few things to discuss."

He stalked toward her. She took a few steps back to retreat from him. Tripping over her feet, she almost fell. Rand caught her, pulling her into his arms.

"This isn't a good idea." Lilliana said. Her breaths came out in small pants. A rosy glow started to form on her cheeks, and her eyes became glassy. All he did was hold her and rub her back gently with his fingers. He wanted her to become accustomed to his arms wrapped around her. They did need to talk before he demonstrated what he came to her cabin for.

"I'm tired of good ideas. I think it's time I did

something I wanted for a change. Starting with how much I want you. I refuse to let you give up on me...on us."

"I already told you..."

"You will not find another lover. You're mine."

"I belong to no one. You best realize that now," Lilliana said with conviction.

"No. You do. You belong to me. And I will tell you exactly why."

"Oh do tell this should be interesting," her reply scathing.

"Because no one else will ever be your equal and because I also belong to you. We are a pair and we belong together. No one else will do for me anymore than any other man will be for you. Stop fighting it."

"Right. Cause I'm the one that's been hiding and avoiding you."

"I'm done. I give up. You said I won, how could I have won, if I don't have you? I'm here and I will show you what it can be like between us."

"You're going to make love to me now?"

He could hear the surprise in her voice and he smiled. "Not exactly. We are going to take this slow. Passion done right is savored. I plan on enjoying every inch of you until you beg for mercy."

"I don't beg."

"You will," he promised.

Pushing her hair aside he caressed her cheek with his lips. Light kisses feathered across her forehead and nose to finally rest on her lips. He tasted her lips with his. Lilliana moaned and pressed her body against him and rubbed her breasts against his chest. He could feel himself harden as her hands roamed across his back. Reaching under her shirt his hand found her breast, and he pinched her nipple between his thumb and finger. He wanted to feel her everywhere. Spinning them around he pressed her against the door and lifted her up.

"Wrap your legs around my waist," he ordered.

Once he had her in the position he wanted, he lifted her shirt and placed his mouth on one of her rosy nipples, and Lilliana groaned with pleasure. He licked and raked his teeth over them until they were pebbled like tiny red berries. He started to rain kisses along her neck and then nibbled on her ear lobe. Her hands pulled at his hair and yanked the silky strands back so she could place her mouth on his. He swung her around, walked her over to the bed, and laid her down. Taking a step back he could see her face flushed with desire and heavy pants leaving her mouth. She sat there staring at him.

"What are you waiting for? Join me."

"No. This is all we are doing tonight. I told you I'm taking my time."

She picked up the nearest object and hurled it at him. It happened to be a heavy book, and he barely dodged before it smacked him in the head instead hitting the wall behind him with a loud bang.

"You are the most frustrating man. Just go before I cause you bodily harm. I hate you."

"No you don't," he said with a laugh. "That's why you're so frustrated. We will continue this at a later time. There are a few things I want from you before we take that final step."

"Too bad. You're not getting them"

"Oh I will. You will gladly give them to me too."

"No, not a chance in hell," she shouted.

"Oh yes, love. I will leave you now. We will table this discussion for when we make port. We should be arriving in South Carolina sometime tomorrow. Good night."

Rand turned and left her to think about his parting words. He would get her to agree to marry him when they arrived. She might not love him yet, but she would. He was willing to settle on passion for now.

CHAPTER ELEVEN

The afternoon sun shined brightly in the sky and beamed down on top of her with brilliance and warmth. Lilliana looked out at the approaching land mass from the deck of the ship. When she decided to shirk her parent's mandates and travel to South Carolina she had never envisioned a journey quite like the one experienced for the past three weeks. Spending time with Rand and getting to know him had been a torturous experience. The man made her feel things she never wanted to feel before. She didn't believe loving any man was a good choice, but here she was letting that unwanted emotion wash over her. Still she didn't want anything of a permanent nature from him. She may have foolishly fallen in love with him, but her views on anything long term hadn't changed. Marriage was still out of the picture for her.

Rand's visit to her cabin the night before had left her hot and needy. She did everything she could think of to get him to succumb to her way of thinking. Nothing in her arsenal had worked in her favor and it might be time to concede defeat. Rand had an agenda of his own and it didn't mesh with hers. Now they were approaching the port of Charleston. Soon she'd be separated from him, never to see his handsome features again. He hadn't given in and become her lover, but perhaps there was a way to still make that happen.

He said he wanted to discuss something with her once they docked at port. There had to be a way to get him to agree to an affair, but she hadn't thought of a means of accomplishing that feat. So with a heavy heart she sighed the closer the ship came to port. No, this journey hadn't gone has she planned at all.

"Why do you look so sad?" she heard Rand say from behind her. "You're almost to your desired destination."

"I don't know what's bothering me. I feel like something good has ended." She wrapped her arms around herself as if to ward off a chill. "There's this feeling of dread that has taken root deep down in my soul."

"It doesn't have to," he whispered in her ear.

She turned around to look into his eyes. Lilliana could see the same anxiety reflected back at her. Rand wanted her, and it appeared like he had some idea on how to make that happen.

"I suppose not," she said.

"I've been meaning to ask you something."

"What's that?"

She had always been a very curious person. Rand needed to get on with whatever he wanted to discuss with her. This hot and cold nonsense was starting to get on her nerves. He needed to just give in already or let her go.

"How do you plan on getting yourself and your trunks to the plantation?"

That's all he had to ask her? Disappointment flowed through her as she let his words crash through her heart. He hadn't wanted to find a way to spend time together. That didn't mean she couldn't find a way to make it happen. Lilliana had a strong will and determination that rivaled any army general. Never had she failed to achieve a goal she set for herself, yet she couldn't help feeling rejected.

"Oh that," she said without enthusiasm. "I sent a

letter on the mail packet before we left, letting them know of my arrival. If everything went as it should the overseer will have a carriage waiting to transport me."

"What will you do if the letter didn't arrive in time?" he asked.

"I don't know, I'm sure I'll think of something."

"Because you always do," he said with sarcasm in his voice.

"Precisely. I can take care of myself."

She watched as he rubbed his temples in frustration. Lilliana knew that she could be a bit vexing and understood his actions. Being aware of her faults did not endear her to his dilemma though; she had her own issues to deal with. Her nature did not allow her to give him any relief. He would need to find a way to work through his aggravation all on his own.

"All right," he finally said. "Let me know if the carriages arrives or not."

"Fine."

"I mean it Lily. I want to know either way so I can see you off."

"Because you care so much about my welfare," she said sarcastically.

"Are you trying to make me angry?" he asked. "I do care about you and you know that. I also want to have a discussion with you before you run off, but I have a few things to take care of before I can have a proper conversation."

"I am just in a mood." Lilliana explained, "I won't run off without talking to you before I leave."

"I need to get back to my crew and help them with the ship. Do you need anything before I leave?" he asked. "Will you be all right if I leave you alone here?"

"Of course, don't be silly. I already told you I could take care of myself. It's not like I'm about to jump ship or something. Go do what needs to be done to dock the ship. I have a plantation to get to later today."

"Okay. I will find you later. Do not leave without seeing me first, promise me."

"I won't, I promise."

If she truly had to say goodbye, she wanted something to remember him by. A kiss she would never forget. They had already kissed a few times but, Lilliana knew she would never tire of kissing Rand. After the first one it had become her favorite activity. If another man kissed her, she knew it would not inspire the same feelings that Rand's did. No man would make her feel quite the same way.

Lilliana enjoyed watching Rand stroll along deck

giving orders to his crew members. He had an authoritative tone in his voice, and they all jumped at his commands. She missed him already and their separation hadn't happened yet. However would she get by knowing she wouldn't see him each morning? A sting of pain hit her chest at the thought of never seeing him again. She couldn't explain the feeling in her chest. Could it be love? Did she go and allow herself to fall in love with Rand? Surely she hadn't been that stupid.

The ship docked at the port in Charleston, and they dropped the anchor. Once they secured the vessel Lilliana only had to wait for them to bring her chests from below. She had already meticulously packed her belongings securely in her trunks. Lilliana scanned the dock to see if anyone from the plantation had arrived to retrieve her. She wanted to get to her new home as soon as possible. No carriages appeared to be anywhere near the wharf. Her heart sank with the realization that she would need to find another mode of transportation to her family's plantation.

Either the letter hadn't made it to the plantation or they didn't have any real idea when the ship was expected to dock. She had only given them an esti-mation of when her arrival would be. Depending on the wind available ship speeds varied making it diffi-cult to determine an exact time a ship might dock at port. Still even with only a broad idea of when to expect her they should still be waiting for her. The overseer would know to account for the variations and make the necessary adjustments. It might be an inconvenience to come and check each day, but that was one of his duties. That must mean the missive she sent got lost or delayed somewhere along the way.

"Did your transport arrive?"

She turned to see Rand standing behind her. Sometimes she thought he had the worst timing, or perhaps the best. He always seemed to appear when she needed his assistance most. After all she wouldn't have been able to sail to Charleston without his aid. It looked like she would now need him to help her find a way to her plantation.

"No. It looks like my message may have been waylaid," she replied.

"Don't worry about it. I had a feeling that this might happen. I will ensure you make it to your destination. It just might take a bit longer than you planned."

"How much longer?" she asked.

"A night perhaps, I will have to arrange for a

carriage to take you to your plantation. In order to do that, I'll have to go to shore and hire one for the journey. I'm unsure how long that will take and I still have a few things to do on board the ship. You are welcome to stay aboard in your cabin or I can escort you to a local inn. If it's possible to take you this evening I will make sure you get there."

"No, don't rush on my account. I can handle one more night on board the ship if you don't mind. I think I'd prefer to stay in my cabin. At least I know what to expect from the accommodations."

It also might give her another opportunity to have Rand as a lover. He wanted to discuss something with her perhaps that was his plan all along.

"Good." He nodded in approval. "I would feel better knowing you are safely on board the ship. You never know what you will find in an inn."

"Thank you for helping me. I know you don't have to."

"Yes, I do. I would never forgive myself if something happened to you, Lily. Your well-being is very important to me."

"I suppose I should make myself comfortable in my cabin. I had hoped to go on land and see a little more of the country I am to call home," she said whimsically.

"If you are willing to stand my company I can take you on a small tour of Charleston when I go to arrange for a carriage. We will have to walk and will only be able to see the downtown area, but I think you will enjoy it. There is nothing like Southern hospitality."

"I'd like that very much," Lilliana said with a small smile on her face.

"Good be ready in an hour and we will go to shore. While we are out we can stop some place for a meal and finally have that conversation. There's something I want to ask you."

"What?"

"Not now Lily, later will come soon enough."

"All right. Come get me in my cabin when you are ready to depart," she told him.

He nodded in assent and walked off to finish whatever a captain needed to once they docked at a port. She admired his handsome face and commanding presence and couldn't wait to spend the afternoon with him strolling along Charleston's streets. Maybe somewhere along the way she would figure out how to spend more time with him. Of course that could be the very thing he wished to discuss with her. She had no idea what his plans included. Hopefully he had something in mind that would allow them to see each other again. Rand may be planning to sail again very soon. Lilliana wanted him to stay with her long enough for them to become lovers, finding a way to make that happen eluded her. No time to worry about what may or may not happen. Lilliana did have one thing to look forward to and focusing on the positive had always been instinctive for her. For now she would go down to her cabin and rest for the upcoming adventure. She had a new town to learn and fall in love with.

CHAPTER TWELVE

The culmination of Rand's life summed up to one thing, loneliness. That realization hit him hard when he discussed it with Lilliana while they were out at sea. Before Lily he had been blind to the reality his life had become. She breathed life into him. He hoped the journey from England to North Carolina had endeared her to him. He believed she wanted him, but was that enough for her to agree to be with him forever? She was an intrinsic part of what he wanted for his life. She held all of his wishes and dreams in the palm of her hands. He knew she wanted to live on the plantation, and he would do whatever it took to make that desire a certainty for her. So with nervousness coursing through his veins he approached her cabin door and knocked on it.

"Come in," she called from behind the door.

Rand walked inside at her bidding. She was sitting on her bed reading a book. Her black curls were falling loosely around her shoulders. Lilliana looked up at him, her blue eyes beaming with questions.

"It could have been anyone knocking. You should have at least gotten up to see who decided to rap at your door," he scolded her.

"It only could've been you. I didn't have expectations for anyone else to call on me." Lilliana shrugged and set the book down next to her. "You didn't have to knock you know. You have an open invitation to visit me any time you like."

Did she still believe that propositioning him would work? He would seriously like to take her up on her offer of just a liaison, but he wanted so much more. He hadn't planned on discussing what he wanted until later. She needed to understand that a love affair would never happen between them. Lilliana deserved everything he had to offer her. He just needed her to accept what he proposed for their future.

"Yeah, I believe you said something similar before," he replied.

"I've been waiting for you for what seems like forever," Lilliana exclaimed. "Why do you keep resisting? We are friends, right? I think that will make us the best lovers because we understand each other."

"No, becoming your lover will make us more than friends. I doubt we could remain anything resembling friendship once the affair ended. If you want to be just friends I suggest you forego the idea we become lovers. It's not something that can be separated. That kind of relationship changes things. I'd want more and you would too. You just don't realize it because of your innocence. Make up your mind one or the other because I refuse to only be your friend. I want a hell of a lot more than that from you."

"Perhaps you could define what constitutes more for you? I don't know how much I'm willing to give."

"More means everything a man could want from a woman. Probably more than even that. I want you to belong to me in every possible way."

Lilliana stood up and walked over to him. She placed her hand on his chest and looked up into his eyes. Her eyes pleaded with him, and it broke his heart that he couldn't be what she wanted him to be. She must understand how it needed to be in order for them to have any chance of a decent relationship. He offered her all of himself and he desired the same from her.

"That may be a bit more than I want. What you are asking of me scares me more than I can express with mere words. I don't give control over easy. If there is a person I could do that with, it would be you. I'm just not so sure I am capable of allowing you to have that much power over me." Lilliana took a few steps away from him putting some distance between them as she spoke.

"I need you Lily. I don't want to change you. I happen to like you the way you are. If you want me, even a little, I need you to take a chance. There is no maybe in this situation. It's all or nothing."

"So I either agree to go along with your plan or you leave me to what? Forget I ever existed? Are you capable of doing that? I don't know if I could ever erase you from my memories. I like you, Rand. A lot more that I thought I could possibly ever like a man. Generally they are worthless to me. Most of them see dollar signs when they look at me."

"And you think I'm like them?" he asked bewildered. "First off, they are all fools if they only see you as a way to gain extra funds. You are the most beautiful woman I've ever met. I see you as a woman not a way to pad my finances."

"Don't act so offended, I meant what I said. I'm very fond of you. I didn't mean to imply you only saw money when you looked at me. I'm just stating how my beaus of the past have viewed me. You are the only male outside of my father and brother that I respect," she told him. "I want you to understand that you are the only male, outside of my family, I could ever possibly trust."

"I see."

"No, I don't think that you do. You mean an awful lot to me Randall Collins. I really do want to attempt more with you. I just don't see that we need to go beyond what I am offering you."

The conversation had derailed, and it looked like he needed to put it back on track.

"I had hoped to convince you that being with me would be not only the best thing for me, but also for you," he replied.

"What do you mean?"

He could hear the anxiety in her voice as the words left her mouth. Lilliana paced through the room and wrung her fingers together. She frowned, and her forehead crinkled up with confusion. Even though this escalated his plans he knew that he had to lay everything out for her—a decision had to be made. If they had a chance of moving forward, he needed her to agree to everything.

"I want to ask you something. I have been thinking about it for a while now," he began. "I know that we both had a different idea of what our future would hold, but I like to think that all changed on our journey."

Lilliana's forehead creased with uncertainty. She remained silent for several seconds before she responded.

"I suppose on some level that is true. What is it that you want to ask me?"

"I think we both have a certain amount of affection for each other. I believe we work well together and could potentially make each other very happy. What I mean is...what I want to ask you..." Rand said his voice shaking and cracked with emotion.

Why did he find it so hard to get the words out? Could he make it any harder on himself? She just stood there in front of him patiently waiting and he stumbled over his words. He just needed to say them and believe she would give him the answer he desired.

"Will you please marry me?" He breathed a sigh of relief as he finally managed to get the words out.

"You want me to be your wife?"

"With all my heart."

Lilliana crossed the distance of the room and stopped directly in front of him. She looked into his eyes and searched for something. He didn't know what, he just knew she was trying to figure him out and appeared to think the answer might reveal itself on his face.

"Why?" she finally asked.

"I thought I explained about the fondness I have for you and how well we are together. We have a spark between us that is dying to ignite. Please consent to be my wife, Lily. I can't just be your lover or your friend. I need all of you."

"You really believe we can make it work?" Lilliana asked. "Because I never intended on getting married. I explained that to you. Why would I have changed my mind? I wanted a lover not a husband."

"I honestly do. I think that we have a better chance than most at making a marriage work," he replied.

"I need more convincing. I don't believe marriage is for me. I need a reason that will make me want to tie myself to you."

She needed more convincing? How did she expect him to convince her? Rand stared at her for several minutes as he weighed his options. He reached down and picked up her hand and pulled her closer to him. With her hand still encased in his, he placed it over his heart and wrapped his free arm around her waist. His heart beat rapidly as he stared into the depths of her blue eyes. Her tongue darted out, and she licked her pink lips, wetting them in expectation. Rand placed his lips on hers and began to kiss her, coaxing her mouth open with fine tuned passion. Lily's free hand began to roam through his hair, tousling it with eager frenzy. He put a small amount of distance between them and began a trail of feather light kisses over her cheeks and down the arch of her neck. A soft moan vibrated against her throat as he caressed it with his lips. Her pulse raced beneath his fingers, and he couldn't tell the difference between the beats of her heart against his drumming rapidly in his ears. Passion ignited fast between them. Their shared ecstasy was never in doubt, only whether or not they would share it for a lifetime.

Rand needed her to agree to be his wife. He hoped that by giving her a small taste she would see that they were meant to be. That this thing between them wouldn't go away after a few times of loving each other. They needed forever to explore each other and the desire that built each time they came together. He released her and backed up a little bit to look her directly in the eyes. They were still flushed with unspoken yearning. He took a deep breath and told her his view on their situation.

"It's time to make a decision. I already explained I require everything from you. I want to wake up each morning by your side and know that you're mine. I want the privilege of making love to you whenever I want and knowing you want that too. If you don't agree to marriage we won't have that. Do you really only want one night? Wouldn't it be so much better to have every night in each other's arms?"

"That does hold some appeal but why would we need to get married to have that. We can still do that without marriage."

"And what if we have children? Do you want them to grow up with that stigma? No. I want it all. Please agree to marry me."

"What about your ships? You said I'd have every night but not if you go off sailing for months at a time."

"I don't plan on sailing again once we are married. There are plenty of men who would love to earn a decent wage and captain my ships for me. I can run the business from here in Charleston and stay with you." Rand caressed her back with his hand. "I used to think the business was all I wanted. Everything I believed about myself changed when I met you. Together we could do anything."

"All right," she said. "You do have a point."

"So, is that a yes?"

"Yes, I will marry you."

Rand pulled her into his arms and held her for a long moment before he felt he could let her go. Leaning down he kissed her forehead and again lightly on her lips as relief pour through his veins. Now that she agreed to marry him, he needed to make it official.

"Good, I'm glad you agree. While we are out we can get married."

"Are you in some kind of hurry? Why do we need to get married so fast?" she asked.

"I don't want to give you a chance to change your mind. Plus I'd like to arrive at your plantation as your husband. Once we get there I want to start our lives together and build something worth keeping forever. I don't see any reason not to begin to make that happen immediately."

"I suppose that makes sense," she said.

"Good, come with me and let's make it official."

Rand grabbed her hand in his and pulled her out of the cabin. They walked up to the deck of the ship and strolled down the gangplank onto the dock. As they roamed the streets of downtown Charleston, Rand couldn't help thinking about the happiness filling him to the brim. She had actually agreed to marry him. For a brief moment, he believed she might say no. That moment of apprehension had made him react with a bit of spontaneity. When he asked her to be his wife his original intention centered around waiting and doing everything right. He panicked and demanded an immediate ceremony for fear she might change her mind. He didn't want to take any chances that she might, with Lily anything was possible. Rand had one goal and it was to make Lily his wife. He didn't have time to worry about anything else, including how her parents would react to their sudden marriage. Viscount Torrington would put him through hell for marrying his daughter without prior permission to do so.

It didn't take them long to find the local church. The church had four long white columns in front of tall burnt red doors. The inside of the chapel had simple designs. It lacked decorations, but had detailed stained glass windows. A man with white hair dressed in the robes of a clergy knelt at the altar lost in prayer. Rand didn't want to disturb him so he led Lily toward a pew and waiting for him to finish his worship. After several minutes he stood up and realized they sat in the pews. He walked over to them and nodded to both of them.

"I am Reverend Thomas," he said. "How can I help you two?"

"We were hoping that you would be willing to marry us," Rand said.

"Certainly," the man agreed. "Did you have a special time in mind?"

"Actually we want to get married right now," Lilliana murmured.

"Really? Is there a reason you two are in a hurry?" he asked.

"Just want to start our lives together. We don't see any reason to wait," Rand responded.

"I guess I can accommodate you. We will need two witnesses," the reverend said. "Do you have anyone in mind?"

"We don't know anyone here in Charleston. We only arrived on my ship this afternoon," Rand explained.

"Well a couple of my parishioners are due to

arrive any minute. We can ask them if they would be willing to stand as witnesses," he said.

"That would be lovely," Lilliana said with a smile.

"In the meantime, why don't you tell me a bit about yourselves? What are your names?"

After Rand gave the reverend their names, they heard a couple walk into the church. They all turned their attention to the new arrivals. An older couple walked up the aisle and stopped by the pew that Rand and Lily were sitting in.

"Jamieson, Eliza glad to see the two of you," the reverend said with a nod.

"We're glad to see you as well Reverend Thomas." Jamieson nodded at him. "Eliza and I are here for our monthly meeting to help the less fortunate in our community."

"Yes, before we begin I'd appreciate your assistance with another matter," the reverend told him.

"What can we do to help?" Eliza asked.

"These two young people wish to get married," the reverend responded. "Would you be willing to stand as witnesses while I perform the ceremony?"

"Oh, how wonderful. I'd be happy to," Eliza smiled.

"I will as well," Jamieson agreed.

"Perfect we have everything we need to begin if the two of you are ready." The reverend looked at Lilliana and Rand.

"We are more than ready." Rand folded Lilliana's hand within his own. "Please begin the ceremony Reverend Thomas."

"Follow me to the altar," he told them.

Lilliana and Rand got out of the pew and walked, still holding hands, up to where the reverend stood. He opened the Bible and began the ceremony to make them husband and wife. The simple wedding appealed to Rand. He liked that they were about to start their lives together without any more complications. They would still have to deal with Lilliana's family at some point, but he wouldn't have changed anything.

"You may kiss your bride," the reverend said to close the ceremony.

Rand pulled Lily into his arms and pressed his lips to hers. The kiss was simple and sweet—nothing like he wanted to do. He had a fierce desire for his beautiful bride, but he knew he couldn't give into those temptations yet. As soon as he got her back to his ship he could have her in every way he wanted. Rand had waited this long, surely he could wait a few more hours to make her completely his. He lifted his lips off of hers and raised his face to look into her eyes. A smile of happiness showed across her extraordinary face. In that moment any doubts he had fell away.

"Are you ready to leave Mrs. Collins?" he asked.

"I am more than ready Mr. Collins."

Rand turned towards Jamieson, Eliza, and Reverend Thomas.

"Thank you all for making sure we were able to have a wedding today. We are forever in your debt." He nodded in their general direction as he spoke.

"Think nothing of it young man. It's nice to see two young people in love and ready to take on the world," the reverend said.

"Nevertheless we appreciate your willingness to perform the ceremony on such short notice. Perhaps we will see you on Sundays for mass." Lilliana smiled at him.

"You are more than welcome to join our congregation," the reverend told them.

"Good day to everyone my wife and I are going to find someplace for a nice dinner."

"Best of luck to you both," the reverend said.

Rand and Lily turned and walked out of the church. Never once did they let go of each other's hands. They found a quiet place to have dinner and patiently waited for to take the next step in their growing relationship. They were now man and wife, and Rand couldn't have planned it all better if he had tried. Lilliana glowed, and he felt himself basking in it as they spent a few quiet moments just enjoying each other's company.

CHAPTER THIRTEEN

a beautiful and enormous feeling swept over Lilliana as she looked at her husband. She shouldn't be surprised by how he made her feel, but every time she looked into his eyes a new thrill rolled through her. She should have expected him to want marriage, but it hadn't really crossed her mind. The more they discussed it the more it had made sense to her. It had taken her a while to admit it to herself, but Lilliana knew she loved Rand. As wonderful as the emotions coursing through her were they didn't compare to the fear of rejection. He hadn't once mentioned his own feelings. Telling him would be a risk, but surely it was worth it.

No matter how many times she let that thought roll through her mind she still had trouble believing it. A husband, she actually had willingly tied herself to someone else forever. For a person that never intended to be anyone's wife so far she found it incredibly easy to be Rand's. Admittedly they had only been husband and wife less than two hours, but everything between them had a natural and oh so right feel to it. Rand hadn't said anything about love in his proposal, and it bothered a small part of her. She needed to know that he loved her, but she would wait until he knew it as much as she did. Forcing him to say the words would take away the joy of them. They wed and for now that had to be enough.

They finished eating their meal and left to procure a coach to take them to the plantation the next day. A small bubble of excitement continued to well inside of her at the thought of them being together in every way possible. She wanted him so much. Nothing could ever change how much she loved him.

"Ah if it isn't the two newlyweds themselves," a male voice said from directly behind them said with a laugh.

Rand and Lily turned to see the witnesses from their wedding directly behind them.

"Jamieson, Eliza," Rand nodded. "We didn't expect to see you two again so soon."

"We just finished our meeting with Reverend Thomas," Eliza smiled.

"It went well, I expect," Lilliana said.

"It did indeed, "Jamieson agreed. "If I am not being to forward, can I ask you a question?"

"Of course," Rand said. "What do you want to know?"

"Well your wife looks mighty familiar to me. Where to you hail from?" Jamieson asked.

"Lily is late of London, England. She's traveling to live at her mother's plantation," Rand replied.

"Actually now it's mine." Lilliana grinned.

"What?" Rand looked surprised.

"It's my dowry. Didn't I mention that?"

"No dear, you failed to inform me of that little bit of knowledge."

"Well now you know," she said with a shrug.

"Oh, I see the resemblance, now," Jamieson said. "You are the daughter of the Viscount Torrington."

Lilliana looked up at him with shock on her face. She didn't think anyone would make the connection from her to her parents. Somehow this man knew not only them, but her relationship with them.

"You know my parents?" she asked.

"I would think so. I am the overseer of the plantation after all. I've worked for your father for years," he replied.

"How serendipitous and quite convenient," Rand said. "We were just looking to hire a carriage to take us to the plantation. Perhaps you can assist us."

"We did get a letter in the post today that Miss Marsden would be arriving shortly. It didn't mention a husband," he said.

"Well as you know that bit was last minute. You did witness the wedding after all. Its Mrs. Collins now," Lilliana told him.

"Indeed we did." Jamieson nodded. "Eliza is the housekeeper at the plantation and also my wife."

"It will be wonderful to have someone living in that big house again," Eliza beamed. "When are you planning on arriving at the plantation?"

"As soon as possible," Lilliana said. "As my husband said, we're looking for a carriage. I have a couple trunks that need to be transported from Rand's ship."

"We can help you with that. We brought a carriage to town. We can meet you at your ship. If you are ready to come tonight you can travel back with us," Jamieson said.

"Oh, that's wonderful. We thought we would have to sleep on the ship again tonight. I'd much prefer a bed that didn't rock quite so much," Lilliana said looking pleased. A joyous smile lit up her face.

"My ship is docked at the port. We can walk back there now and meet you to load the trunks onto your carriage."

"A solid plan young man. We will meet you there shortly," Jamieson answered.

Lilliana and Rand started to walk back to his ship. Once there, Rand began to order a couple of his deck hands to get Lily's trunks ready to be taken to the awaiting carriage. Lilliana leaned on the railing of the ship and surveyed her surroundings. Nothing about the day had gone as she imagined it. She found herself wed and heading off to her plantation to start her life anew.

"Are you ready to go see your plantation, dear," Rand said from behind her.

Lilliana smiled as she turned and wrapped her arms around him. She rested her head on his shoulder and for a brief moment just enjoyed the feel of his arms wrapped around her.

"Yes," she told him. "I feel like I've been waiting forever to get to where I am right now."

"We haven't arrived just yet."

"I know, but we will soon. This journey has been about more than reaching the plantation. It's also about me and what I want out of life. Thanks to you I'm realizing all of my dreams. I owe you so much."

"You don't owe me anything," he said with a shake of his head. "You have it all mixed up. It's I that owes you."

"We will have to agree to disagree," she responded.

"I have a feeling we will be doing that a lot in our lifetime."

"You may have a point," she said with a laugh. "But for now let's go to the plantation. I would like to arrive before nightfall."

"I would as well."

"Which reminds me. Did something about Jamieson seem familiar to you?" Lilliana said.

"Not particularly," Rand said.

"I don't know what it is just yet, but he reminds me of someone. I'll figure it out when I've had more time to think about. With all the excitement of the day my mind can't stay focused on one thing."

"I'm sure you will." He leaned down and placed a soft kiss on her forehead. "Let's go join them in their carriage."

"All right," she said.

Lilliana walked down to meet Jamieson and Eliza at the carriage. Once they arrived Lilliana took a moment to observe them. They were an older couple around her parent's age. "Have you been taking care of the plantation the entire time that my parents have been married?" Lilliana asked them.

"I took over shortly after your parents were married," Jamieson told her. "I used to work with your father."

"Please tell me you didn't sail with him in his pirate days," Rand exclaimed.

"Actually I used to be his first mate," Jamieson said.

Lilliana heard Rand groan at Jamieson's admission. She really didn't see why. So what if Jamieson used to be the first mate on her father's ship. That didn't make him a bad person, but perhaps she was a bit biased. She adored her father and didn't think that the fact he used to be a pirate detracted from his lovable nature.

"Oh that's wonderful. You will have to tell me some stories from when you two sailed together." Lilliana asserted.

"Well, I must admit the most interesting one involved your mother." Jamieson explained.

"I know he kidnapped her. Father used to tell us the story of how they met as a bedtime story."

"Are you serious?" Rand asked baffled.

"Of course I am. I wouldn't joke about such a thing. Their story had a very romantic element to it," Lilliana told him.

"He kidnapped her!" Rand shouted.

"What's your point?" Lilliana asked. "It led to them falling in love. You do realize I wouldn't exist if that hadn't happened."

"I do." He sighed. "That doesn't make what he did right."

"Perhaps not, but my father would never hurt my mother." She folded her hands over her chest, staring into his eyes. "Everyone is human Rand. We are all capable of making mistakes. He owned up to his and my mother forgave him. It isn't our place to judge."

"You're right, of course. I just can't wrap my head around it."

The carriage rattled along the narrow road as they talked. The journey toward the plantation amounted to a few miles outside of Charleston. Talking as they traveled helped the journey go faster, making it seem like it only took minutes to arrive.

"Well lad, the little lady is right. Thor loves Pia. That fact became evident pretty fast to the crew. If you take out the things you find atrocious it did have a romantic feel to it," Jamieson told him.

"I will have to take your word for it," Rand replied.

"Jamieson, have we met before?" Lillian asked.

"Only once, when you were about five or six years old. Your parents traveled to make sure that the plantation's assets were okay after the end of the war. You all stayed for a few months. Your mother was a bit reluctant to leave. You liked it so much that was when she declared it would be part of your dowry."

"I didn't know that. My parents never told me why they made it part of my dowry," Lilliana said. "You seem so familiar to me though, I don't think that brief meeting would have left an impression."

"No ma'am I doubt it would have. I barely saw you on that visit. I spent most of my time with your parents making sure they had all the information they sought."

She couldn't put her finger on what was so familiar about him. Lilliana was determined to figure it all out. Spending time with Jamieson and Eliza on the plantation would help her ferret out the mystery. She had time to figure out why he was so recognizable to her. Perhaps it was just because she had met him before, but she doubted it.

CHAPTER FOURTEEN

The carriage pulled to a stop in front of a large plantation house with four large white columns encasing the entranceway. The house was entirely white with large windows and two large green front doors. A wide staircase led to the porch and entranceway. Rand could see why his wife wanted to live in the plantation home. It was a piece of beautiful architecture with a rich history. The fact that it had survived the war was an amazing feat. He couldn't wait to start his new life in this home with Lilliana.

Jamieson hopped down from the carriage once it was at a complete stop. First he helped Eliza down from the carriage, and then he began to reach for the trunks strapped down to the back of the carriage.

Rand helped Lily from the carriage and turned to speak to Jamieson.

"I can help you with those," Rand said.

"If you are willing to help me get these up to your room I'll be much obliged."

"Most of this stuff does belong to my wife. I'd be an awful cur to leave it for you to do alone."

"I'd understand if you wanted to get settled in right away. I'm sure the journey here was quite lengthy. I appreciate your help." Jamieson nodded at Rand in appreciation.

"The faster we get these unloaded to sooner we can all relax. I'm sure you'll appreciate a little extra time to unwind."

"I do indeed. Let's get these trunks inside," Jamieson proposed. "It'll be dark soon."

Jamieson reached over and pulled the straps off of the trunks and began drag it over so it would be easier to lift. Rand stepped over by the other side. They each stood by their chosen side, lifted, and walked the trunk indoors. Rand let Jamieson lead him up the stairs to the room he would share with his wife. Once they reached the room they set the trunk by bed and went to retrieve the other trunk.

"Those trunks are a lot heavier than they look,"

Jamieson said once the trunks were delivered to their room.

"I have no idea what she has in any of them." Rand laughed and wiped a bead of sweat off his brow. "I am not sure I want to know either."

"Can't say I blame you. Sometimes it's best to be left in the dark."

Rand laughed again. "You may be right there."

"I am, trust me. I've been married twice and I learned the hard way not to question certain things in a woman's boudoir."

"What happened to your first wife?" Rand asked. "If I'm not being too personal that is."

"No, no it's okay. It's been a lot of years since my first wife died. I gave up on the domestic side of things after I lost her and our child. It took a lot for me to get back on my feet. Thor played a huge part in making me want to live again. Meeting Eliza made me realize I could allow myself to be happy. My wife, I loved her dearly, and I know she wouldn't have wanted me to throw my life away because she died."

"I'm so sorry. That had to be very difficult for you. I'm sorry I made you relive it even for a small moment. I couldn't imagine what I'd do if I lost Lily."

"I hope it doesn't come to that." Jamieson's face

became solemn. His eyes took on a darker hue as he frowned.

Rand hoped speaking of his deceased wife and child wouldn't leave him in a melancholy mood for the rest of the night. He hated that he may have caused him any misery. Unfortunately he could relate on a small level. Growing up as an orphan gave him firsthand knowledge to the wretchedness of losing a family member. He never wanted to experience that heartache ever again. At the sound of Jamieson's voice he snapped back to the present. He couldn't let the despair of the past wrap its way around his heart again.

"Let's go downstairs. It's time for dinner and I'm sure Eliza has a wonderful meal prepared for us," Jamieson said.

The two of them left the bedroom and strolled down the stairs. Rand followed Jamieson to the dining room. They went inside the room to find Lily laughing at something Eliza had said. She looked up at him and her smile grew brighter. She motioned for him to come closer and take the seat next to her.

"Is everything all taken care of?"

"Yes. The trunks are stored up in our room."

"Good. I can unpack tomorrow," she said.

"That's a scary thought. Those trunks were quite heavy."

"I had to take what I deemed important. I don't plan on returning to England anytime soon." She shrugged.

"Yes. I can see why taking things that you needed and deemed important would top your list. If there is anything you need that you didn't bring with you please let me know."

"I don't need you to provide for me, Rand. I can take care of myself."

"I know you can, but you're my wife now. It's my privilege to see to your wants and needs. I look forward to it all."

"It feels a bit controlling to me." Lily's left eyebrow lifted widening it so the blue of her eye was more noticeable. Her cheeks flushed a pretty shade of pink as she pressed her lips together forming an appealing pucker.

"I didn't mean it to be. Forgive me?"

"You're forgiven." Lilliana leaned over and wrapped her arms around him to give him a quick hug. "I know you didn't mean it the way it sounded. Sit down and eat something. I'd like to start our first night as husband and wife on a good note."

He intended to have a beautiful wedding night

DAWN BROWER

with her. He had an idea on how he could make it both beautiful and wonderful. With a firm plan set in his head he sat back to enjoy the meal.

"It looks like you have prepared a lovely meal, Eliza," Rand said.

"It does indeed," Lilliana said. "If you don't mind me asking what do you call all of this?"

"We eat a light meal in the evenings. Our big meals are usually served at noon. This is just a simple meal of corn bread, frizzled beef, stewed fruits, and oyster pie." Eliza replied.

"It all looks delicious," Lilliana said. "I can't wait to sample everything."

"We also have tea or milk if you'd like," Eliza offered.

"I'll have some tea please. I haven't had a decent cup in ages."

Rand laughed. "She acts like the crossing over on my ship deprived her of the niceties in life."

"Nonsense, I had a lovely time aboard your ship. I just haven't had tea since the morning we left England," Lilliana replied. "I'm quite looking forward to a nice cup of it. If it's not too much trouble that is."

"You should know Mrs. Collins..." Jamieson began to say.

"Lily, please," she interrupted. "You've worked with my father. You can call me by my given name. My closest friends and family call me Lily. I insist you do as well."

"Lily," Jamieson began, "I received a letter from your father. I just got a chance to look over today's post."

Rand stopped eating and looked up as Jamieson spoke. It couldn't be good news he had to impart. Viscount Torrington had to be out for blood since Lilliana ran away from home. He would be in his crosshairs for assisting her in her act of defiance. Something he was not looking forward to, but knew it would be a necessary evil if he wanted to make peace with the man.

"That doesn't surprise me," Lilliana said. "What did he say?"

"He is coming for a visit. He mentioned that you might show up before him and I needed to make sure you didn't leave before he arrived."

Lilliana laughed before saying, "Why ever would he think I'd leave? I told him in the letter I left for him and mother I planned on residing here."

"Wait a minute you left them a letter? You didn't tell me that," Rand exclaimed.

"I didn't?" Lilliana answered. "I swear I mentioned it."

Rand rubbed his temples as he let her words wash over him. How could she have forgotten to mention that little tidbit to him? Didn't she believe he had a right to know something so important? "No dear, I'd have remembered you telling me that you left your ex-pirate father a letter telling him you had run away from home. In fact, you said earlier that you intended to write them once you arrived at the plantation."

"Hmmm...well I guess I do remember saying that. I didn't know how you would take it. It's not important really. I gave it to Gemma to give them once they realized I hadn't gone to stay at her country estate." Lilliana paused and looked him in the eye. "I had to do it, you know that."

"Yes, I do. I'd have just preferred knowing that you had." Rand sighed.

"Oh I see, you think I deliberately left you in the dark? Which I suppose you are right about. I had intended on letting you know at some point though. It slipped my mind. Whenever you are around me I tend to forget important matters, for more desirable ones. In my defense you never once asked for any details on what I had in the works."

"You are right once again, I didn't ask, because I really didn't care at the time," Rand agreed.

Lilliana flashed him a brilliant smile.

"I did say we would have to deal with your parents at some point."

"Indeed you did," Lilliana looked over and asked, "Jamieson, did my father give you any idea when they might arrive?"

"I'd give it a rough estimate of within a day of your arrival to a week depending on the weather for their crossing."

A day? That wasn't nearly enough time to prepare for the arrival of his wife's parents. "So it's a possibility for them to show up sometime tomorrow." Rand sat back in his chair and awaited a response to his question.

"It is," Jamieson agreed.

"We will just have to make sure we are ready for their arrival. I'm sure Torrington will want my head when he arrives," Rand replied. He folded his hands under the table and began clenching and unclenching them. He didn't want her parents to dislike him, but he didn't regret marrying Lily.

"I'm not likely to let him kill you, lad," Jamison replied.

"Nor I, as I rather like your head where it is,"

Lilliana agreed. "I really don't think you need to worry though, they will be happy I decided to get married. They have been pushing me towards matrimony for a while now."

"I have to agree with you. I'm rather attached to my head myself." Rand nodded at his wife. "I have to disagree with you though; we have plenty to be worried about. I know if my daughter married some random man I'd be out for blood. Just be prepared for the worst."

"I'd rather not dwell on it to much. Let's make plans for something fun instead." Lilliana said changing the subject.

He didn't want to cause Lily any stress so for her sake he would attempt to let it go. He knew she was being too nonchalant about it though.

"You could go horseback riding and learn the land you inherited," Eliza suggested.

"That's a lovely idea. Do you have horses here that we can ride tomorrow?" Lilliana asked.

"Yes, there are a few in the stable suitable for riding. I can help you when you are ready to leave," Jamieson replied.

"After breakfast we can go for a ride. Does that work for you Rand?"

"I think it's a fine idea."

"Wonderful. It will be nice to be able to ride a horse again."

"There you go picking on my ship again," Rand said with a laugh.

Lilliana stuck her tongue out at him with a playful laugh in return.

"I have fond memories of your ship. I am not the one picking on it."

"I know, dear. I'm just giving you a hard time." Rand moved to get up. "If you will excuse me, I'm tired and going to go rest in my room."

"I can come up with you," Lilliana said.

Rand stiffened at her offer to join him, but he didn't want her to come along with him just yet. He had plans for their special night. He would welcome her willingly later on, eagerly.

"No, finish your meal. Join me later. I'm not going anywhere, I promise."

Rand left them in the dining room and bounced up the stairs to the room he shared with Lily. He had an idea on how to make their first night together as husband and wife unforgettable. He needed a few things and everything would be perfect. Lilliana deserved the best and he intended to make sure she had it.

CHAPTER FIFTEEN

*L*illiana sat as long as she could with Jamieson and Eliza, trying her best to enjoy the food before her. It all tasted like grains of sand. What she wanted was to join her husband in their room. The food did nothing to quench her needs. Only Rand would be able to accomplish that. She had no idea what Rand was up to, but she intended to find out.

"If you will excuse me, it's time I retired. It has been a long day." Her patience had its limitations and she found herself at the edge of them as she looked over her supper companions.

"Of course, have a good night. We'll see you at breakfast," Eliza said.

Lilliana nodded at both of them as she got up

from the table. She walked out of the room and with a slow gait strolled up the stairs. The staircase was wide and open with plush red velvet cascading down each step. The baluster and newels were burnt mahogany, polished to a perfect shine. The hallway wove down an intricate path that led to several bedrooms. She remembered where hers was because she loved it so much. It was located at the end of the hall on the left. The room was decorated in a mint green and browns. It reminded her of a decadent forest.

When she reached her destination she opened the door and gasped in surprise. The illumination from all of the candles bathed the room with a soft glow. Lilliana looked up and saw her husband's desire filled gaze. He had removed some of his clothing and sauntered to her side in his bare feet. Lilliana stared into his eyes as he reached up and caressed her face with one of his hand. His other arm wound around her waist and pulled her toward him.

"I've been waiting for you."

"I'm here now," she said as she licked her lips. "If you had given me a clue I'd have been here sooner."

"I don't mind. The best things are worth waiting for."

"You say the sweetest things," she whispered.

"I don't. I say what I mean." He placed a small kiss on her neck. "I feel like I've been waiting for you my whole life."

"You don't need to wait anymore. I'm here, take everything you want."

"I intend to. Now that I have you exactly where I want you, I am going to take my time...and savor every inch of you."

He leaned down and pressed his lips over hers in a light kiss. Lilliana released a small breath filled with anticipation; Rand pressed his lips more firmly to hers. He tasted wonderful, like honey and cinnamon. She let her tongue duel with his for control. Their passion escalated the longer they kissed. Lilliana raised her arms and wrapped them around his neck and pulled him closer to her.

He pulled away and looked down at her. Lilliana bit down on her swollen lip and moaned. If he didn't start giving her what she needed she had no problem forcing him to her way of thinking.

"Take it easy, love," he whispered as his lips caressed her ear. "We have all night to explore each other."

"I need so much..."

"So do I, but it will be so much better if we take our time."

"I don't want to. Please Rand."

She ran her hands through his hair and pulled his head towards hers. Their passion ignited full force. Lips, tongues, and teeth battled to get the upper hand. He turned her around and pressed her against the wall; Rand unlatched every hook of her dress and pulled it down. She didn't wear a corset so she stood before him in only her chemise and pantalettes. She could feel his body towering over her as his hands roamed her body. He continued to place little kisses along her neck and shoulders.

"I'm going to take every last stitch of clothing off of you now, Lily." His breath hot on her ears as he whispered, "Then I'm going to taste you everywhere."

She felt herself grow wet between her legs at his words. His words evoked so many different tumultuous emotions inside of her. Her skin was sensitive to his touch; every place his hands roamed she grew hotter, needier, and more desperate to see what he would do next. Rand peeled the rest of her clothing of as fast as possible and turned her back around to face him. He took a step back and let his gaze roam over her nude body. Lilliana's body heated to a scorching flame under his direct scrutiny. Looking boldly into his eyes she reached up and cupped both of her breasts in her own hands and pinched her nipples. She saw him gasp with a sharp intake of breath and slowly release it. Her desire escalated the longer he watched her.

She wanted to reach out and touch him; more importantly she wanted him to remove the rest of his clothing so she could look at his gorgeous body.

"You are stunning and you're mine."

He took a step closer to her and reached out to touch her naked body. His hands roamed over her naked breasts and plumped her nipples between his fingers. They became stiff from his ministrations, and he drew one of the nipples inside of his mouth. His tongue roamed over it and brought a long drawn out moan from her mouth.

"Please Rand, I need you."

"And I will give it to you, love. Together we will do and feel so much tonight."

He pulled her with him to the bed and laid her down with gentleness on the soft mattress. His gaze caressed her again before he lay down next to her on the bed. His hands trailed over her belly and brushed over the curls between her legs. His nimble fingers found her center as they rubbed her tender flesh.

Lilliana ached so much and needed him to be inside of her. She didn't understand why he didn't make her his. He seemed to be moving too slow for her and, she had no clue how to make him go any faster. She didn't know what to expect having never made love to man before, but Rand made her want and need everything he did with her. Every sensation trailing over her body made her ache for him in so many ways.

He changed positions and crawled over top of her. He lowered his face between her legs and pushed her legs further apart. She didn't know what he intended until his lips kissed the nub between her legs. She would have squeezed his head with her legs if he hadn't been holding them in place. His tongue rolled over her sensitive flesh and she screamed.

"So beautiful," he said before he lowered his head again and started to lick her core.

The more he licked the tighter her body got in anticipation. Rand's gaze held hers for a moment as he watched something wonderful build within of her, a pressure so deep that at any moment an explosion would occur. She couldn't help being frightened by the intensity while secretly hoping for something more. He continued his relentless strokes of his tongue on her hypersensitive center. She didn't know what happened inside of her but she knew if he didn't stop she'd burst from all of the sensations. Her intuition proved right as she ruptured from the inside out. Her body quaked with uncontrollable spasms, and she screamed with each new ripple of pleasure outpouring from her body. Nothing had ever compared to what he just made her feel. She wanted to feel it again.

She looked up through hazy eyes as he undressed. Finally she would be able to see his beautiful body. Once all of his clothes were removed, he joined her on the bed again. His shoulders, chest, and arms were rippling with well-defined muscle. Light patches of hair dusted his chest and trailed down to his stomach. She looked at his thick manhood and wanted to wrap her hands around it. She couldn't help but wonder how it would fit inside of her. Every inch of him appeared too large, and she feared her body wouldn't be able to accommodate him. She really wanted to try though because she had a need building up inside of her. One she knew only he could fill.

"I think you are ready for me now," he said.

"I've always been ready for you."

"I know and we're going to do things a little differently," he whispered. "Do you trust me?"

"Always."

He rolled her on her side with her derriere facing him. He lifted her leg, pulled it over his hip and with slow thrusts started to enter her from behind. Her tight channel didn't want to let him in, but she desperately needed to feel all of him inside of her. She leaned back as he slid himself inside of her one slow inch at a time. When he reached her barrier he stopped for a moment to allow her body time to adjust, and then pushed fully inside of her. Lily's heart filled with so much love to have him joined with her. Even the brief sting of pain was worth it to know how it would feel to have him deep inside of her. She never thought she could feel so much emotion welling up inside of her. A small tear formed in the corner of her eye as her own happiness overwhelmed her. Rand waited for as she became accustomed to being filled by him, and once the ache left she started to move against him. Having him inside of her was beyond her wildest imagination. The completeness made her feel whole and part of him.

"Easy love. There is no need to rush."

"Please, Rand. Love me."

"I do, I am."

He continued to push himself in to her until he

filled her completely. The completeness of his filling her had been amazing, but it didn't compare to his strokes caressing her channel. The different feelings he caused as he thrust himself in an out of her couldn't be explained. As he rocked himself inside of her, he also caressed her with his hands and lips. He pinched her nipples and rubbed them with the palm of his hands. A thousand tiny sensations roared through her body, and she knew she would explode at any minute. Just before her body detonated he leaned down and absorbed her scream with his mouth. Her core squeezed him, and she felt his seed burst within her. He wrapped his arms around her and groaned as he kissed her wild abandon.

"Lily, you undo me," he said as he trailed light kisses over her forehead and cheek.

"No more than you do me."

He slowly pulled himself out of her. Emptiness overcame her at the loss of him. She wanted more and as soon as possible. The reality of loving him had far surpassed anything in her wildest dreams. Rand got out of bed and blew out any candles still lit then crawled back in bed tugging the covers over top of them. He left a lantern lit on the bedside table to extinguish itself as the fuel burned out. He pulled

Lily into his arms and held onto her as if his life depended on it.

Lilliana couldn't sleep. Emotions filled her to the brim in a turbulent fashion. She had trouble stilling them long enough to relax and fall to sleep. She could hear Rand's even breaths as he slept beside her. She wondered how he could remain so calm as her own emotions jumped all over the place. Lilliana needed him to know how much he meant to her.

"Rand, are you asleep?" she asked quietly.

No answer came from him. She found it incredulous he could sleep at a time like this.

"I guess you are," she said as she snuggled closer to him. "If you were awake I'd tell you how much you mean to me. I'd let you know that you changed me. I know that you don't love me yet, but I can love you enough for the both of us. In time I know you will love me too. You just need to allow yourself to feel it. I can wait for you."

She closed her eyes and took a deep breath.

"I can wait because you are worth waiting for. I just wish you stayed awake to allow me to say this all to you. I'm going to do it again when you will actually hear me." She caressed his cheeks lightly with the tip of her fingers. "I don't mind telling you I love you a million times."

With a smile on her lips she opened her eyes to gaze at his handsome face. Yes, she could and would do whatever it took to make him feel how much she loved him. For now she would lose herself in some much needed sleep. The morning would arrive soon enough and she could tell him that fact over break-fast if needed.

CHAPTER SIXTEEN

*R*and held Lilliana tight. He heard every word she said the night before. He just hadn't known how to respond to them. Rand no longer had a lonely feeling roaming through his soul. Lilliana's confession had meant so much to him. She had given him a gift he didn't think he could ever return. He didn't feel worthy of her love, but he was selfish and would not refuse it. He needed her and would never let her go. Lilliana fit into his life perfectly—in a way he never knew he needed. She gave him a new purpose, and he intended to make sure she never regretted gifting him with her love. After she fell asleep, he watched her all night. A more beautiful sight didn't exist for him. His wife had sneaked into his heart and seized it when he let his guard down. She owned his soul.

While his gaze remained on her she rolled over and opened her eyes. "Good morning," she said and rubbed her eyes with her hands.

"Good morning to you beautiful." He gave her a quick kiss. "Are you ready to start your day?"

"Can't we just stay in bed all day, I can think of a few things we can do," she said coyly.

"Well I never said we had to get out of bed just yet." Rand kissed her again.

She wound her arms around his neck as he deepened the kiss. When he lifted her leg around his hip, he could feel her wetness stroke his shaft. The need to be inside her grew as his cock hardened. He trailed kisses down her neck and he pushed himself inside of her. She moaned with pleasure. With slow strokes, he slid in and out of her tight channel until her breaths became heavy on his shoulder. She bit his ear and licked away the pain.

"You feel so wonderful inside of me," she said with a groan. "Give me more Rand. I need it."

At her words he began to move harder and faster inside of her. A squeal of pleasure filled the room as he rolled Lily on her back and raised her hips under his hands. She wrapped her legs around his waist and held him tight against her. He rode her hard until she screamed as her orgasm rolled over her. He followed her into bliss a short time after her.

Rand held her tight in his arms when each wave of pleasure reached in and grabbed a hold of his soul. He rolled them onto their sides with heavy breaths coming out of his mouth. His breathing started to slow down and even out as his body became more relaxed. He didn't think loving her could get any better, but this time the pleasure had been even more intense than the first time.

"Darling, I do believe you have found your calling."

"And what's that?" she asked with boldness in her voice. Her fingers trailed lightly down his back.

"Loving me," he said and kissed her forehead.

"Always."

"I hate to say it, but I do believe we need to start moving now."

"Must we?"

"Yes, Jamieson and Eliza are expecting us for breakfast and we did make plans to go horseback riding. Unless you have changed your mind about getting a look at this land you inherited."

"I do want to go horseback riding. So let's start the day."

"Good. Let's get moving. I'm famished."

"So am I," she said with a laugh. "And yes, for food."

They got up and quickly got dressed. Rand grabbed Lily's hand as they strolled down the stairs into the dining room. Eliza and Jamieson were already seated at the table. Jamieson had a paper spread out in his arms as he read it. Eliza sipped from her cup as she gazed at nothing in front of her.

"Good morning," Lilliana said them both.

Jamieson closed his paper and looked over at the two of them as they sat down at the table. Rand nodded to him.

"I trust you both slept well," Jamieson said.

"Indeed we did," Lilliana said as a small blush grew on her cheeks.

It did his heart good to see that his wife could be embarrassed. He believed her brazen attitude over-flowed every aspect of her life.

"Can I get you two any coffee or tea?" Eliza asked. "We have a small breakfast bar and we serve ourselves. There are hard-boiled eggs, sausages, and toast. A variety of jams as well as some scones if you like."

"I'd like some tea," Lilliana answered.

"What about you, Mr. Collins?"

"Coffee, and please call me Rand. I don't see why we should remain formal."

"Thank you," she said with kindness. "I don't see any reason either. I will get your drinks and be back soon."

He watched as she left the room. Eliza was a kind woman. He liked to think his mother would have been like her.

"Would you like me to make a plate for you?" he asked Lilliana.

"Oh, that would be lovely, thank you."

"Anything in particular you want?"

"A bit of everything," she said with a laugh. "I did tell you I'm famished remember."

Rand got up to make a plate for himself and Lilliana. As she requested he put a little bit of every-thing on her plate before he set it in front of her. He decided he would do the same for himself as he finished filling up his own plate. He sat down at the table and took a bite of toast as he looked over at his wife.

"Are you still planning on taking a couple of horses out today?" Jamieson asked.

"Yes we are. After we finish breakfast if that's still all right." Lily said.

"Of course it is. Technically you do own them after all."

"I guess I do. I hadn't thought of that," she answered.

"When you are finished, I will walk out to the stable with you and show you which horses are good for riding," Jamieson said.

They ate in silence as Rand watched Lilliana eat everything he had put on her plate. She really had worked up an appetite. Once she finished eating she dabbed her mouth with her napkin and looked over at him.

"What?" she asked.

"Nothing, just admiring my wife."

"We'll I'm done eating and want to go riding. Are you finished?"

"Eating? Absolutely."

"Well I guess we are ready to go investigate that stable of horses," Lilliana proclaimed.

"If you'll follow me I will show them to you," Jamieson replied.

A door slammed and a loud noise rumbled through the house followed by an equally thunderous bellow.

"Lilliana Marsden, where are you!"

"I think your parents have arrived." Jamieson said

with a tilt of his head. "I believe that bellow was your father."

They looked up as they saw Viscount Torrington storm into the room followed by a woman that Rand assumed was his wife and Lily's mother. Viscount Torrington's face was so red it bordered on being purple. If Rand were a coward he would try to slink out the door, and out of harm's way. He didn't back down from anyone and he planned on staying married to Lily for the rest of his life. If he had one hope it would be a very long life. He could have gone a while without dealing with her father, but it looked as if he didn't have much choice in the matter.

"Young lady we have some things to discuss." Torrington glared at Lily as the words roared from within him.

"Are you hungry father? We were just enjoying breakfast. Please have a seat," Lily replied with a cajoling voice.

Rand suppressed the urge to roll his eyes at Lily and her father. Did she really believe treating him like a child in the throes of a temper tantrum would work?

"Don't try to placate me young lady. You deliberately disobeyed and lied to us. You will answer for your indiscretions." Torrington practically bellowed the words at her.

Rand's lips formed a thin line of displeasure. He understood Torrington's irritation, but he couldn't and wouldn't allow him to lay a hand on her. Lily was his to protect now. "Well, I can't allow you to punish her. Please have a seat Viscount Torrington so we can discuss the situation like civilized people." Maybe if he reasoned with her father they could handle the situation as peacefully as possible.

Torrington turned and glared at Rand. Up until that point his attention had been solely focused on Lilliana. He knew that he would have to face him eventually, and it looked like it was time to do so. Rand had no regrets even if it looked like the man intended to beat him to a bloody pulp.

"I think I understand now." Torrington stormed over to Rand's side of the table and leaned on one of the chairs. "You are the one I need to hold responsible. Why did you kidnap my daughter, Mr. Collins? Did my interpretation of your business make you that mad? I don't take those actions lightly."

Rand should have known that the viscount was entirely too calm as he stood there talking to him. He believed the man capable of reasoning, but he should have factored in Lilliana's importance to him.

If he had a daughter he would have been capable of murdering the poor sot that ran away with her. He didn't blame the man for his feelings on the matter. However the fist that planted in his face and knocking him out he did find fault with. *The blasted man hadn't even let me explain anything* was his last thought before blackness took over and he fell unconscious.

CHAPTER SEVENTEEN

*L*illiana jumped out of her chair and ran around the table to kneel before Rand's crumpled body sprawled out on the floor. At first she had remained rooted in her seat in horror watching her father's fist meet Rand's face. It was only after her mind could process the scene before her she was able to act. A scream to match her dismay erupted from her mouth before she rushed to her husband's side. Now she patted his cheek lightly to see if she could get him to wake up without any success.

"Jamieson, we need to get him upstairs." Lilliana gasped. "I don't know how long he is going to be out."

"I can certainly help. Thor, you are going to need to help me, he isn't a small lad."

"Damned if I do. I think he's exactly where he belongs."

Lilliana turned and glared at her father. His only reaction was to shrug without care. Her father may believe Rand belonged on the floor, but it was only because he didn't really know him. In his mind he kidnapped her forcing her to accompany him to South Carolina.

"Don't be an arse. He likely deserved to be pummeled a bit for running off with your daughter, but he is now her husband. You need to respect that." Jamieson spoke up to her father.

"In fact, I don't. I plan on murdering the thieving bastard as soon as he wakes up. He clearly had a death wish and I'm happy to oblige," Torrington replied.

Lilliana could see from the expression on her father's face he meant every word he said. She had to find a way to reason with him. The blame belonged squarely on her shoulders, not Rand's. The decision to run away had been made long before she had met him. She needed to make him understand how much she loved Rand. She adored her father, but she was not going to allow him to harm her husband. No matter what it took she would make sure her father understood he couldn't come between her and the man she loved.

"Daddy, I can't allow you to hurt him any more than you have. Please understand this decision was mine to make, not yours. I belong here with my husband." She walked over to him and placed her hands in his. She looked up into his eyes and showed every ounce of emotion rolling through her in one look. Lilliana pleaded and demanded with her eyes for her father to understand what she wanted from him. If he couldn't hear her words she wanted him to see what his actions would do to her. "I need your help. Can you try to recognize that and assist Jamieson to take him up to the bedroom?"

"Fine. I will help him, but then you and I are going to have a long overdue talk."

Lilliana turned to Jamieson and said, "Can I trust you to make sure no harm comes to him while you both take him upstairs?"

"You have my word, the lad will arrive safely. " Jamieson nodded at her father. "I will make sure he comes back down with me after we settle him in your room."

"I'm not going to do him any harm." He glared

down at Rand's unconscious body. "Not until he is awake at least."

He walked over and grabbed Rand's head and heaved upward as Jamieson grabbed his feet. She noticed that even though her father had agreed to help carry Rand he didn't do it with any kind of care to his well-being. It irritated Lilliana to watch him be so disrespectful to her new husband. She would just have to take Jamieson at his word. He would make sure her father didn't hurt him. Once they came back down she would make sure her father understood what would happen if he did anything at all to her husband. She would never speak to him again if he marred him in any way.

"I think we need to talk before your father comes back down."

Lilliana turned to look at her mother. She had barely noticed her arrival after her father forced his way into the dining room. Breakfast was completely ruined. She had lost her appetite anyway when she watched Rand fall from his chair and hit the ground with a loud thud.

"I think you may be right. I've made a mess of things," Lilliana said with a sigh.

"Darling, that is the understatement of the year." Her mother rolled her eyes as she pushed a strand of her pale blonde hair behind her ear. "You didn't have to deal with your father for the past three weeks. I don't think I've seen him this mad since my grand-pere tried to murder him."

"Your grandpere actually did that? I thought that was just something you made up to make the story sound more daring."

"Yes, he did and don't change the subject. You need to explain yourself. Why did you run off? Did meeting that man cause you to lose your mind?" her mother asked.

"No of course not. Don't be ridiculous. I didn't leave because of Rand. He just made it possible for me to get what I wanted."

"Then explain this all to me. Why did you marry him? I know you were against marriage."

"I'm not allowed to fall in love? I didn't leave because of him. I left because I wanted to live here. You were just not listening to me. So I made the necessary arrangements to get what I wanted. Rand just agreed to transport me." Lilliana walked over to her mother and grasped her hands within in her own. "He's an amazing man, Mama. I'm not saying that just because I love him. He protected me and made sure I had everything I needed. Even when I threw myself at him he refused me. He's a good choice and I stand by it."

"Well you don't have to convince me. It's your father that isn't likely to believe you. It might take a little bit to make him understand, but I will try to help you."

"Thank you. I am sorry that I worried you. I tried to alleviate that."

"When you have children of your own someday you will realize a mere letter isn't reassuring enough. Parents always worry about their children. It's a responsibility that never goes away."

"I need to check up on him," Lilliana said.

"Your father isn't likely to let you near him until he has words with you. I've never seen him so irate and scared at the same time. Thor always seems to have things under control. Let him have his say first. I'm sure your husband will be fine in the meantime."

"I suppose you're right. I will wait." Lilliana looked over at the open doorway. "However, I'm not going to let him scream at me while my husband needs me. I will give him a moment of time to say his piece, but if I think Rand needs me the conversation is over."

Right after those words left her mouth Thor breezed in followed by Jamieson. He still wore a thunderous expression on his face. His lips pursed in displeasure, and his eyes narrowed to tiny slits as he focused his attention on her once again.

"Now that I've tossed the rubbish into another room, you and I are going to have a little discussion on mistruths and nearly giving your parents heart palpitations."

"I already apologized to mom. I'm extending it to you as well. You know I didn't mean to make you worry about me. This is where I want to be. I'm sorry, Daddy, but this is where I belong."

"You wouldn't be here if not for that upstart American. I can't believe you married him. We can rectify that when we get home."

"Are you listening to me at all? I'm not going back to England. Not now and probably not for a long time. I married Rand of my own free will. Nothing you say will make me want to leave him. I love him and I'm staying here as his wife."

"I'll tell you how I will rectify it. I will make sure the bloody bastard is no longer breathing."

Lilliana flinched as those words left her father's mouth. How could he threaten the man she loved? Didn't he want her to fall in love and get married? Both her parents kept pushing her toward that end, and now he doesn't like the result? No, her father would understand he couldn't dictate to her any longer, and he would never lay a hand on her husband again.

"You will do no such thing. Rand hasn't had an easy life. You are not going to make it any more miserable. He grew up alone in an orphanage. His mother died giving birth to him. He told me he knows next to nothing about his parents. I know it pains him that he didn't know anything about her except her name."

"Your daughter has a point, Thor. You need..."

Her father interrupted Jamieson, "I don't need to do a bloody thing. You have no idea what I went through when I found out she hopped a ship with him. I've never been so scared in my life."

"I think I understand that kind of pain better than anyone," Jamieson replied quietly.

She heard her father groan so she turned her attention back to him. He had a perplexed look on his face as he watched Jamieson.

"I'm so sorry—I wasn't thinking. I know you experienced a loss that would cripple even the strongest man."

Lilliana bobbed her head back and forth between the two of them. "I don't understand what you are talking about."

"I lost my first wife, Emily, and our child. She died giving birth to him. The poor boy wasn't breathing when he came out. I lost everything in one moment and wasn't even there to see them both through it."

"Emily? How interesting, that's Rand's mother's name," Lily replied deep in thought. She couldn't help wondering if there was a connection. Could there be? No, Jamieson said they both died. She grabbed Jamieson's arm and gained his full attention. "I don't mean to pry, but is there maybe a possibility—"

Her father turned toward Jamieson and asked, "Do you know what she is talking about?"

"Are you suggesting what I think you are? How could that even be possible?"

Lilliana wasn't sure if she hoped she was right, or if she prayed she was wrong. She could see pain in every inch of Jamieson's features. "What was your Emily's full name?"

"Before we married it was Emily—" Jamieson paused for a second and rubbed his hand over his face, "Good God, how did I not see it?"

"See what?" her father asked.

"Her name was Emily Collins...they both share the same name. Do you think they did it on purpose? Gave him her family name to hide him from me?"

Her father shook his head and shrugged. "I'm not sure, Jamieson. I don't have the answers you seek, but surely this is a good thing. You have a son."

"Only a few decades too late," bitterness laced Jamieson's voice.

All this information was a little too much for her to take in. Jamieson was Rand's father. No wonder he seemed so familiar to her. Lilliana stared at him for several moments. She took in all of his features and mannerisms. The more she looked at him the clarity of it all became firmer inside of her head. She knew why Jamieson seemed so familiar to her. It should have been obvious from the start. He reminded her of her own husband. It all made sense now that she had all of the information. How was she going to tell her husband about this? It was all so —extraordinary.

"Who do you think hid him from you?" Lilliana asked.

Her father placed a hand on Jamison's shoulder, giving him support. Her father knew something she didn't. He must have been privy to this story. They were close; they sailed on a ship together. Jamieson must have shared the details with him.

"Her damn family. When they found out she was pregnant they disowned her. I arrived after she had given birth to him. They told me she died and that the baby never even had its first breath. How could they have lied to me?" Jamieson crinkled up as pain poured out of his eyes. A small sound of pain fell from his lips before he spoke again. "I grieved so much that it led me to signing on to work with Thor on his ship. Nothing could have kept me in Beaufort after that. No one knew she was really my wife and wouldn't tell me anything. Told me it was a family affair. I didn't much see the point in fighting them. I believed I had nothing left to live for."

"Rand is your son. Why would they do that to their own grandchild? They may have hated you, but Emily was still their daughter," Lilliana said bewildered.

"Not everyone sees things in the same way. She ruined herself by getting involved with me. They believed her soiled goods. I don't know why they lied about my son dying. I would ask them if they were still alive. That is if I could stop myself from strangling them."

"I get why this information is interesting to Jamieson, but explain to me why you even care Father."

Lilliana understood why Jamieson was a bit emotional at the news, but her father seemed equally overwhelmed. Not too long ago he was out to murder her husband. Something that still irked her.

"I can't very well murder my friend's only child. Especially as he just found out he existed, now can I?"

"Oh, I see how you are. You can murder my husband, but not your friend's son. That is some convoluted logic." Lilliana's blood boiled at his statement. She clenched her hands into tight fists and restrained herself from hitting her own father.

"I have to agree with her there, Thor. That doesn't make much sense to me," her mother interjected as she walked into the room.

Lilliana turned to look at her mother. At least she had one reasonable person on her side. "Thanks Mother, though I could have used your support a lot sooner."

Her mother waved her hand in dismissal. "I came in when I was needed. Have you settled everything?"

"Father was just going to explain why it made a difference that Rand is now Jamieson's son, not just my lowly husband." Lilliana glared at her father. "I'm not so sure we've settled anything."

"You didn't watch him suffer when he believed

they both had died. It's personal and I also under-stand what it's like to be a father now." Her father folded his arms over his chest. "Although I can't kill him, it doesn't mean I can't maim him a bit. He did abduct my daughter."

Jamieson frowned and said, "Well from what I understand of the situation she left rather willingly. You can't harass the lad for helping her out. Besides it isn't like you didn't do a little kidnapping in your day."

"He does have a point dear," Pia agreed.

If the situation wasn't completely ludicrous Lilliana would laugh. How had things gotten so far out of hand? She hoped Rand took the news all right that he had a father. It probably wouldn't help having to deal with her father as well. It would be some pretty difficult news to swallow on top of all the chaos already in their lives. At least her father wouldn't murder him now. She still thought it was absurd he only decided against that action because Jamieson believed Rand to be his son.

"Well, you two keep discussing this nonsense. I'm going to go check on my husband."

With those words Lilliana stormed out of the room to go check on Rand. Maybe he was awake now and she could spend some time with him. He did say he would take her horseback riding around the plantation. Of course that might be asking a bit too much, she would let him decide what he was capable of doing. If all he wanted was to go for a sedate walk she'd do it. She was just grateful to have him in her life. Maybe that would be a good way for them to get away from the madness that had overtaken everyone.

$\mathcal{R}$ and woke up in his room with a splitting headache courtesy of his new father-in-law. When his head cleared he walked down the stairs to confront him. No way did he intend to leave Lilliana to fight his battles for him. When he reached the doorway he overheard them discussing his mother. Everyone always said you never heard anything good when you eavesdropped. He learned that lesson the hard way. Rand tromped away from his wife—and his father.

With the earth-shattering news—Jamieson being his father—dropped on him, he needed to get away and think. Rand practically ran out the front door to gain some distance between him and his newfound family. The only thing he thought about as he strolled away from the house was how much his life changed in such a short period of time. He didn't notice where his feet led him; he just kept prodding along until he couldn't take another step. When he finally took notice of his surroundings he saw a large oak tree looming in front of him. Its branches blew in the breeze as the leaves whistled with each movement.

His breaths became shallow as he swallowed that truth with a heavy reluctance. He never expected to find the man who helped create him. So many emotions rushed through him he couldn't pinpoint which one to hold onto. He needed to get back to the house and be there for his wife. He knew he acted like a coward by walking away. Closing himself off and not dealing with the issue wouldn't solve anything. He should have stayed and faced his demons instead of running at the first sign of adversity.

Jamieson seemed like a good man, aside from working as a pirate's right hand man. If what he said held true then he didn't know of his existence. Rand couldn't hold him accountable for the actions of someone else. He should give him a chance to be the father he never had. Easier said than done, in his opinion at least, years of believed abandonment were hard to let go of. He knew Jamieson said he thought he died. Rand heard all of the details; it was just hard for him to process. He wanted to believe everything he heard, but it all had a surreal feeling to it.

He had more than himself to think of now. With a heavy heart he started back toward the house. Lilliana depended on him, and he couldn't let his own inner turmoil get the best of him. As he walked back up the plantation steps, Lilliana exited the house and stopped with the door open. She stared at him for several minutes before she stepped forward and wrapped her arms around him.

"I'm so sorry. My father shouldn't have hit you."

"I don't blame him, Lily, he should be protective of his daughter."

"Still. He could have at least listened first before reacting." Lilliana frowned.

"I don't want to talk about it. I just want to hold you for a little while."

"There is something I should tell you..."

"I already know."

She was going to tell him about Jamieson. He didn't want to discuss his newfound father with her. He wanted to forget he had overheard the conversation.

"You do? How?"

"I overheard part of the conversation. It was a little bit to take in. It's why I'm outside. I needed the fresh air. To think," he said in a quiet tone.

"I see. I'm at a loss on how to respond. I thought you were out here because of me and my father. Instead it has to do with the news about yours. How does it make you feel?"

"I don't feel like talking about it. Why don't we go for a ride instead. It is what we planned before your father rudely interrupted us."

"Shouldn't we ask Jamieson..."

"Ask me what?"

They turned to see Jamieson standing in the open doorway. Rand wanted to walk away again. He didn't want to deal with him and what the man could mean for him. He did want to make his wife happy so he tried to put a smile on his face just for her, even though smiling made his face hurt.

"We are looking to go horseback riding." Rand said.

"Ah, I'd hoped to talk to you. I went looking and you were not in your room."

He wanted to give him a chance, but he hadn't had enough time to process it all. Jamieson may mean well—he just couldn't handle his well meaning emotional responses at the moment ."I'm not much in the mood to talk right now."

"It's kind of important, son."

"Don't call me that. I'm not your son," Rand replied scathingly.

"Rand!" Lilliana's shock evident on her face. "I don't think you need to be so rude to Jamieson. He is only trying to reach out to you and talk."

"You know?" Jamieson asked.

"That you believe you are my father? Yes. It doesn't make it true," Rand said.

"If your mother is—was Emily Collins, then yes, I am your father," Jamieson said with conviction.

Rand stood and looked at the man for the first time and took him in. Jamieson's features resembled his in a lot of ways, and he carried himself with an air of authority. Looking him over it didn't surprise him as much to realize that the man claimed to be his father.

"I know you think this is some kind of miracle. I'm not so blind to the ramifications of this mess. I'm not going to hug you and say I'm glad you are my long lost dad. I'm not made like that. I can't just accept you and be okay with years of perceived abandonment."

"No one is expecting you to... Just give it some time." Lilliana wrapped him in a tight embrace.

"Just show us the horses. I can't deal with this right now."

"I can do that," Jamieson agreed.

They strolled to the barn, and Jamieson led them to two horses in stalls next to each other. They were beautiful well-mannered animals.

"The chestnut is named Max and the white filly we call Sally. They are both good horses and are great for riding. Do you require a side saddle?"

"No, I don't ride side saddle," Lilly told him. "I have a skirt made just for riding astride, it splits down the middle. I made sure to wear it when I got dressed this morning anticipating going horseback riding."

"Good, I don't much care for the side saddle, it's dangerous," Jamieson replied.

"My father agrees and never allowed me to learn how to ride with one."

"I'll help you two get the horses saddled so you can be on your way."

Jamieson opened the stall and threw a saddle up on one of the horses. Lilliana stood to the side as Rand put the saddle on the other horse. Once both horses were prepared, they mounted them and rode them out of the barn. Lilliana's laugh of delight filled the air as she brought the horse to a light canter. Rand caught up to her quickly and kept up with the pace she set.

"I think we should talk about what happened," Lilliana said.

"I'm not ready to think of him as my father, Lily. Don't push it."

"You really need to give him a chance, but it's your decision I won't push."

"Thank you for supporting me."

"I'm your wife. It's what I'm supposed to do." She smiled. "How about a race?"

He started to tell her to no, but she took off at a fast gallop before he could get the words out. He knew she was only trying to lighten his mood, but he deemed a horse race too dangerous. No way would he put her life at risk by galloping their horses at full speed.

"Slow down Lily," Rand called.

His heart thundered in his chest as she sped in front of him. He wanted to reach out and stop her, but it was physically impossible. Rand could feel the color draining from his face with each bit of distance that grew between them.

She didn't hear him call out to her. Lilliana kept her horse's pace at a fast gallop. Rand raced to catch up to her, but she had gained a terrifying lead. She turned her head to look back at him, and with her attention divided she didn't see the tree branch directly in her path. She turned a moment too late, and Rand screamed as she flew from the horse. Her body hit the ground with a loud *thud*. He stopped his horse and jumped off of it racing to her side. Fear like he never knew before spread though his body. He couldn't lose her, not when he just found her, not ever. A tear began to form in his eye and fell down his cheek as he knelt beside her still body. Pain began to seep into his heart at the thought of losing her.

"Oh Lily, please be okay," he said pulling her into his arms. "I love you, I can't lose you when I just found you."

He stood and carried her back to the house trying not to jostle her. His fear was palpable and deep rooted inside of him. He had never been so afraid in his life. When he saw her flying from the horse all of his worst nightmares came to life.

"Quick someone help me, Lily took a nasty fall from her horse," Rand yelled.

Just as the words left his mouth he heard a voice

bellow, "What the bloody hell did you do to my daughter?"

"I didn't do a damned thing to her, she fell from her horse. Help me take care of her."

Torrington reached to take Lilliana out of his arms, but Rand refused to relinquish her over to him.

"I'm not handing her over to you, she's fine where she is and I'm taking her upstairs until a physician can look at her."

Rand could hear them discussing the situation as he walked with huge steps toward their bedroom.

"Thor leave the man be, can't you see how distraught he is?" He heard Lilliana's mother say, stopping Viscount Torrington from going after Rand.

"He's manhandling my little girl."

"Sorry Thor, but I have to disagree with you again," Jamieson said.

"On which part, ol' friend, the manhandling or the fact that she's my little girl?" Thor asked.

"Well both actually. What I see is a man looking out for his wife."

"I fail to see your point." Thor's angry voice bellowed through the plantation walls.

"Rand and Lily are married. Sorry, Thor, but I believe that trumps your rights a bit."

"Bloody hell, I need a drink," Thor cursed. "What the hell are you waiting for, my daughter needs a physician. Send for one already."

Even though Rand had fear coursing through his body a small smile formed on his face. He heard Thor storm into the sitting room. At least Jamieson had his back. Maybe he could accept him in his life if the man willingly stood up to an ex-pirate.

CHAPTER NINETEEN

*P*ain crashed through her skull as someone poked at her body. Tiny shards of agony filled her head with every touch. A constant thrum of torment beat against the back of her head, and every inch of her body was stiff with soreness. Whoever thought it a good idea to add to the throbbing burrowing its way inside of her would soon find the error of their ways. She didn't do well with any kind of discomfort, and the idiot kept adding to it with each poke and prod he made. If only she could open her eyes to tell him to stop stabbing her with his fingers. Her eyes refused to open, but she could hear everyone around her.

"She's just unconscious," she heard someone say.

"I expect she'll be in a lot of pain once she wakes up. Her body is one huge bruise."

"But she will be okay?" a familiar voice asked.

Rand. He wanted to make sure she would be okay. *Of course I will be,* she wanted to scream the words at him. He shouldn't be made to worry about her.

"She better be all right, boy," another familiar voice roared. "Or I'll make sure you take your last breath."

Her father threatened her husband again. When would he stop tormenting Rand? Her mother had to be nearby; she wouldn't leave knowing Lilliana was hurt. Why hadn't she said something? Lily needed to hear her mother's voice.

"You won't be murdering my son, Thor. Back off."

Ah, yes, Jamieson would be there to help support Rand. Happiness filled her at the sound of Jamieson's voice. Rand had someone in his corner. He needed someone on his side. He often let the weight of the world hold him down. Jamieson would make sure he didn't give into his darker side.

"He's right, Thor. You are only making things worse by threatening him. Be happy that Lily chose him. You know we thought she'd never get married. I'm happy she found someone to give her heart to."

Oh yes Mama, I did. He's wonderful! I can't wait for you to know him as I do. She needed to wake up and tell them everything. The pain in her skull throbbed harder and faster as it tried to beat her from the inside out. *Please stop I can't take the pain anymore.*

"There are too many of you in the room," a man she assumed was the doctor told everyone. "Only two visitors at a time or she'll never get enough rest to heal."

"Fine. Everyone can leave. I want to spend some time alone with my wife."

Good for you Rand. Tell them all to leave. It should just be you and me for a while. My head hurts and I can't think with all of them hovering over me.

She heard some rustling as a door opened and closed. She believed that all of them left the room without arguing with Rand. That made things easier on both of them. The silence was blissful and the pain began to ease a bit as it washed over Lilliana. She could feel a head lay down on her waist and grabbed a hold of her hands. It must be Rand. He wouldn't have left her. He must have found a chair to set by the bed so he could keep vigil. She needed to wake up and help ease his pain.

"I will keep you company," Jamieson said.

So she was wrong. Not everyone left the room.

Jamieson stayed behind to be with Rand.

"I'm fine. I don't need you."

"Yes son. I believe you do. You don't have to do everything alone."

"I've done it alone all my life. I don't see why I should change that now," Rand said in a bitter voice.

"Right now I'll remind you that you are not alone. You have me and Eliza if you want us, but more importantly you have a wife," Jamieson said. "I'm so sorry son; I wouldn't have abandoned you if I'd known you lived."

"It couldn't be helped. You didn't know. And you're right. Lily needs me. I can't let this eat up inside of me."

"I would never hurt you intentionally."

"In my head I understand that, but my hearts been bruised beyond recognition. I didn't allow myself to feel anything for anyone until I met Lily," Rand said.

"If you give me a chance, I'd like to get to know you."

"I don't know. Give me some time to let it all sink in."

"I can respect that. I hope you give me a chance. Eliza and I were never blessed with children. Since I missed out on raising you, I'd like to have a chance at being a grandfather."

"I can't make any promises. Right now I'd like to be alone with my wife."

"All right. I will leave you be for now. She will get better Rand."

Lilliana heard the door open and close again. Jamieson had left. The only ones in the room were her and Rand. She needed to open her eyes and let him know she would be okay.

"Lily, love, please wake up," he pleaded.

I'm trying! I would if I could.

"I love you, I should have told you sooner I know. I just couldn't get the words out. Last night I heard everything you said. I wish I could have spoken then. Please hear me now. I need you to know how I feel. I have never had these strong feelings before."

I knew you loved me! I hear you Rand, I hear everything you are saying to me. I just can't seem to open my eyes. It hurts too much. Give me some time. I can do it I know I can.

"You are also right about my father. I do need to give him a chance. It's just so hard for me to accept anyone in my life. I've been alone for so long. I can't be alone anymore. Wake up Lily. Please don't leave me."

"I love you," Lilliana said with a hoarse whisper.

"Did you say something?" he asked with desperation.

"You heard me," she barely got out the words before he pulled her into his arms with a fierce hug.

"Can you open your eyes, love?"

"Hurts...too...much."

"That's okay, you should rest."

"My parents..."

"I can get them for you, if you want," he said.

"Yes, please. Need to speak to them." Lilliana croaked out, her voice hoarse from being so tight and dry. She struggled to get them out and let her Rand know what she wanted.

"I'll get them now. Just relax as I retrieve them."

Lilliana heard him leave the room in a rush. It seemed like hours before they finally came up the stairs. She must have drifted off again because when she opened her eyes only her mother sat at her side.

"Where's Daddy?" she asked with a hitch in her voice.

"I'm over here, princess."

Lilliana turned her head slightly to see her father standing by the window in her room. The afternoon sun streamed through the glass. Her father had a troubled look on his face.

"So happy to see you both," she said.

"You gave us quite a scare, young lady," her mother said. Her blue eyes held an enormous amount of concern and warmth. Her forehead crinkled up as she spoke. Her pale blonde hair was in disarray, as she must have run her hands through it with worry. "What were you thinking?"

"I wanted to make Rand smile. He looked so sad when he found out Jamieson was his father. Instead I ended up with a cracked head. That'll teach me for galloping at such fast speeds."

"I'm glad you are okay. I've never been so scared in my life." Her mother leaned down to hug her. "That doesn't make what you did right. Don't ever do something so foolish again."

"I know and I'm sorry, forgive me."

"Always, princess, we can never stay mad at you, but did you really have to go and marry Jamieson's only son? Right now I'd really like to murder him for putting you in danger," her father said.

"Be kind Daddy. I love him."

"I'll try. I'm not happy about it."

"I know, I promise you'll get used to the idea in time."

"I will make sure he plays nice," Pia said and

kissed Lily on the cheek. "In the meantime you need your rest."

"Rand..."

"Is not so patiently waiting for us to leave." Pia smiled. "There isn't supposed to be more than two of us in the room at a time. Rand said you wanted to see us both which left him standing in the hallway."

"I did. I heard you talking. I had to make it right." She could barely keep her eyes open, and they were tiny slits as she looked at him. She fought the struggle her body demanded of her. She refused to succumb to the sleep her body required to heal. She needed to talk to them and make them understand. If she let herself doze back off she wouldn't be able to take care of her immediate concerns.

"You did, princess." Her father leaned over and kissed her cheek. "Don't worry about us. Just concentrate on getting better."

She watched her parents walk to the door to leave.

"I love you both. Thank you for being such wonderful parents."

"The pleasure, princess, belongs to us, you were one of our blessings. We couldn't have asked for a better daughter."

Rand entered the room immediately after they

left and sat down by her side. He lifted her hand to his mouth and placed a quick kiss in her palm. Her husband had been put through a lot in a very short time, and she didn't have a clue how to help him through it all.

His hazel eyes had held so much pain as he looked at her. She would have done anything in her power to ease it, but he hadn't given her a chance. Rand had done a good job of acting like he would be okay, but she knew him better than that. He may have laughed a little and acted untroubled, but she knew inside it shredded him. If he needed a little bit of time to himself to ease the hurt within, then she would ensure he had it.

"Did you say everything you needed to them?"

"Yes, I believe I did."

"I'm glad."

"What about you?"

"I don't know what you mean," he said.

"Have you talked with your father?"

"I had a small talk with him while you talked with your parents. We have a long way to go, but he knows I'm willing to try and build a relationship with him. I talked with Eliza as well. She cried a little bit and hugged me. It turns out she isn't capable of having children of her own. She wants to consider me her son. It's not a huge step, but it's a start. It's all I can offer them right now."

"Well that's good for you. You now have two wonderful people to call your parents," Lilliana said.

"I know it is, but it's still not going to be easy for me. I don't know what I'm doing here. It's all new territory for me."

Lilliana looked into Rand's eyes and just enjoyed gazing into their depths for a few minutes. He had such a sensitive nature, but didn't know how to express it.

"You will be fine. Besides you will have me every step of the way."

"I know. If I didn't have you by my side I wouldn't be able to do all of this. I wouldn't even be here to know who my father was. I owe everything to you. Thank you for agreeing to be my wife, Lily."

Lilliana needed to lighten the mood a bit. It had taken a turn she didn't want to go down just yet. She didn't need his gratitude, but she'd gladly take any love he'd willingly bestow upon her.

"I had my own selfish reasons for marrying you, you know."

"Oh yeah? What were they?" he asked with a smile.

"I knew you wouldn't be able to keep you hands

off of me if I happened to be your wife." A hushed chuckle filled the room.

"I knew you were a wanton from the moment I met you."

"Really, do tell, what gave me away?" she asked with coyness.

"You had a devilish smile and you knew how to lure in your prey."

"So you are now my prey? I didn't know I had such power."

"You hold all the power, Lily. You are my life. I'd be lost without you. Do not ever do anything like you did earlier today. I thought I died a million times seeing you lying on the ground."

She could imagine how that scared him. If it had been in reverse and he lay on the ground hurt, she'd have been frantic. If she had a way of doing it all over again she'd never get on the horse.

"I didn't mean for that to happen, I'd never hurt you."

"You can be a bit reckless at times. Its part of why I love you so much, but it scares me at the same time."

"Is that all you love about me?" she asked.

"No, I love everything about you. I adore how your eyes fill with that devilishness I spoke of earlier, I admire your tenacity to get what you want, cherish the way you fight for those you care about, I worship the ground you walk on, but mostly I just love you with every beat of my heart."

"Oh Rand, I love you too. You have a great capacity for love. I knew it from the moment I looked into your eyes. It's why I knew you were the right man, not only to take me to Charleston, but to welcome into my life forever." Lilliana reached up and caressed his cheek with the palm of her hand. "You are the reason I changed my views on marriage. Because of you I started to believe love existed again." Lilliana paused, and looked down at her lap. A lump of emotion welled up inside of her. Once she regained control she looked up into Rand's eyes. "When I first started to socialize in society the men hadn't inspired me to believe in it. None of the ton marriages had been based on love. They only married for some kind of gain, either financial or power. I never wanted a marriage based on such low expectations. I always knew I wanted more. I thought my parents' marriage was a rarity and love only found the lucky few. I'm glad I'm among those blessed with it."

Rand leaned down and brushed her lips with his. At that moment she wished she hadn't cracked her head so hard on the tree branch and on the ground. She wanted to show him exactly how much she loved him, but her body hurt too much.

"I wish we could make love, but it would be too painful," she said with a bit of whimsy.

"We have the rest of our lives to express our love to each other, it can wait for you to heal. I want to be able to love you over and over. As soon as you are ready we are going to spend a whole day in bed doing just that. In the mean time you will have to settle for a few brief kisses and caresses."

"You're going to torture me, aren't you? That will be your revenge for me scaring you so badly. Admit it."

"You know me so well, love. I have to get my kicks in somewhere." He laughed.

Lilliana stuck her tongue out at him.

"I will get even if you do."

"Promise?"

"Always."

With that, Rand got up and lay down next to her in the bed. Lilliana curled up next to him and rested her head on his shoulder. A small sigh escaped from her at how good it felt to be in his arms. They had come a long way in a few short weeks. They loved each other and had a long happy life ahead of them.

Rand treasured her as much as she did him. Lilliana belonged with Rand, their love made them stronger. They could face anything as long as they did it by each other's side. Lilliana couldn't have asked for a better beginning to their story. More importantly, Lily couldn't wait to have children of her own. It would be her turn to craft a fairytale. She would tell her children a tale of true love, much as her father had with her and Liam. It would start with, *Once upon a time a lady asked a gentleman to help her run away...*

EXCERPT: A SANGUINE GEM

A MARSDEN ROMANCE BOOK THREE

DAWN BROWER

CHAPTER ONE

*L*iam Marsden had a lot of things on his mind. However, he couldn't dwell on what was beyond his control. He had more pressing issues to deal with, starting with a meeting his father demanded. He had never let him down before, and he had no intention of starting at this juncture of his life.

He walked into his family home and strolled down the hallway towards the study. As he opened the door, he got a brief look at his father engrossed in his own work. The viscount had his dark hair pulled back at the nape of his neck; loose strands fell over his forehead as he tilted his head to read the paper in front of him. Liam had always admired his tenacity and willingness to do anything to accomplish any task. He didn't give up easily and believed the world belonged to him to take what he wanted from it.

"Ah good you're here," He glanced up at Liam and set his work aside. "I have a few things I need to discuss with you."

"I came as soon as I received your missive. What's so urgent?"

"A good number of things that I didn't foresee."

On closer scrutiny, Liam could see stress lines forming on his father's face. His eyes filled with worry as he rubbed his temples. What could have happened to make him appear so concerned? Liam didn't think this meeting would be a jovial one. His father didn't often worry about things. No, Viscount Torrington took action and left the fretting to others.

"This is serious?" Liam asked as he raised an eyebrow.

"I received a letter from your sister. Some of it is good news. Most of it is actually."

"It's the part that isn't good news that concerns you." Liam sat down and leaned forward, giving his father his full attention. "What has happened?"

"First, I should tell you that you are the proud uncle of a strapping baby boy. You sister had her child a month ago. They named him William Jamieson after his two grandfathers. Poor boy has a lot to live up to with that name." He laughed.

"If I'm an uncle that means you are a grandfather. How does that make you feel old man" Liam grinned. He couldn't resist an opportunity to tease his father.

"Bite your tongue, boy. It'll be a long time before I'm an old man," With a devilish grin on his face, his father sat back in his chair and studied Liam. "This is good for you because I don't think you are quite ready to fill my shoes."

Liam hoped his father lived a very long life. He couldn't imagine a life without the man's robust personality filling a room wherever he went. Like most children, he believed his parents infallible. He knew they were mere human beings, but he liked to believe they would live forever.

"No, I can't say I'm in a hurry to take the reins from you. I pray you're here for many years to come. For more reasons than one," Liam said. "But regardless of how I feel about your possible demise that isn't why you summoned me here. Nor is it the news about my new nephew. Grateful as I am to hear about it, something else weighs on your mind. I think it's time to dispense with the pleasantries."

"That isn't all your sister wrote about," he said with a heavy sigh. "She has some concerns that she asked me to look into."

"Is it about the merger of Marsden Shipping with RandCo? There isn't an issue with its completion, is there?" He needed to dispense with that bit of concern first because it was at the forefront of his mind. "If so, I'd like to take care of it immediately."

"No, that at least is going well. We should have considered a merger as soon as Lily and Rand married." Viscount Torrington sighed and stood up. He strolled over to a nearby shelf and pulled out a decanter of brandy along with two glasses. "This is something entirely different and I'm not sure how to proceed."

"What's Lily worried about?" Liam's concern rose. What could be so dreadful?

Viscount Torrington handed Liam a brandy filled snifter. He took a sip of his own and set it down. He stared past Liam, his eyes unfocused. "The Earl of Devon was a pretty good friend of mine."

"I remember." Liam nodded.

"At one time I'd hope to have a merger with him," his father paused and stared down at his drink. "It was the reason we attempted to betroth you and Gemma."

Liam would rather forget about that time in his life. He grimaced and stared up at his father. "Right, that was several years ago." What was his father getting at?

"The business merger and familial one fell through at the same time. We never found a reason to revisit either." He downed the rest of his drink in his glass. "I have to admit a part of me is glad it didn't. As much as I liked the man I abhor the gentleman who inherited his estate."

Liam rubbed his temple; a pain throbbed through his head listening to his father rattle on. "What does Alfie have to do with this?"

"Lady Gemma is my concern."

She wasn't his, so Liam had no clue why he brought her into the conversation. In fact, everything he'd said so far hadn't made any sense to him.

"Father, what exactly is the problem?" Frustration built to the boiling point deep inside him. "I don't understand what Lady Gemma has to do with all of this."

"Lady Gemma keeps in touch with Lily. She wrote your sister about some disturbing news." The viscount sat back and studied Liam. He steepled his hands together as he spoke. "She thinks I might have a solution to the problem. I can think of a couple of ways we could assist her, but you would have to be willing."

"What it is you would like me to do?" Liam replied, a horrible feeling sinking to the bottom of his gut.

Viscount Torrington leaned forward and set his hands on his desk. His eyes bore into Liam's as he appeared to weigh over the issue that troubled him.

"You know I'd never force you to do anything, but I think in this you believe as I do."

"I'm at a loss as you haven't explained anything to me," Liam reminded him. "How am I to know if I agree or not if you don't?" He silently hoped his father wasn't about to ask what he thought he was. After he mentioned the botched attempt to betroth him to Lady Gemma, Liam couldn't help but wonder —he couldn't possibly want him to marry Gemma. *Could he?*

"First, you should be aware of the circumstances regarding Lady Gemma and why Lily is so concerned," his father told him. "Then I will explain my idea and the two possible solutions to it. One is a better option, and the other should only be considered if you are against the first."

"And what is happening with her?" Liam stood up and paced around the room. He stopped a few steps away and pinned his father with a stare. "Quit stalling and tell me what's going on."

"Alfie is—being difficult."

"In what way?"

If his father didn't tell him what was going on soon. Liam wouldn't be held responsible for his actions. Their conversation was driving him mad.

"He has squandered the entire inheritance. If the estate weren't entailed, he'd sell it to pay off his enormous debts. That leaves him in a bit of a bind. He needs money and as fast as possible."

Liam nodded. "I think I see the correlation. Lady Gemma still has an inheritance, and he wants to get his hands on it."

Viscount Torrington stood up and joined him in front of the desk. His eyes had an angry edge to them. Liam knew his father well enough to realize he wanted to do some damage to the new Earl of Devon. Whatever Alfie was doing enraged him. Liam had a bad feeling about what was going on with Lily's friend.

"In a manner of speaking yes and he is willing to use whatever is at his disposal to get it. Lady Gemma is afraid he might force the situation to get his way."

"I see." Liam scowled. "Does she have reason to believe he will act so dishonorably?"

"This is old news." His father frowned and crossed his arms over his chest. "I got the letter today from your sister. It might already be a foregone conclusion. I'm afraid we may be too late with how slow mail travels between England and America. I don't know what we'll find if we go to the Earl of Devon's estate."

Not good news, in fact, they were quite horrid. Liam might have issues with Lady Gemma, but he'd never wanted anyone to hurt her. He'd willingly help her deal with her cousin if he could find a good solution to her problem.

"I hadn't even considered that. We are wasting time. What are your solutions?" Liam asked.

"Lady Gemma needs a husband. She doesn't gain majority and control over her funds for five more years. She only has one solution that will effectively work for her."

With those words, Liam's fears were realized. His heart beat faster in his chest and the pounding in his head intensified.

His father wanted him to marry Lady Gemma.

Liam should be appalled at the suggestion, especially as he'd already tried to betroth them when they were younger. He had never denied that Lady Gemma had beauty in spades. She had luxurious crimson hair and eyes the color of jade. His mouth watered thinking about her beautiful complexion and soft curves. That was until she open her mouth to speak. Listening to her droll on and on for what seemed like forever, he invariably forgot how exquisite her body and face appeared and wanted to put some much needed distance between them.

Why should he sacrifice his life for her?

The brazen redhead had been the bane of his existence for several years now. It took the death of her father for her to back away. Admittedly he admired her tenacity and willingness to make her wishes known, but that didn't mean he ever desired to tie himself to her forever. Perhaps his father's other solution would be easier for him to stomach.

"You are not suggesting what I think you are." Appalled, Liam sat back down in his chair. Shock filled him to the brink. He had to be reading the situation wrong.

"I had hoped that you had some tender feelings for the chit. You are constantly arguing with her." His father sat back down in his chair, a slight knowing smirk resting on his face. "That is a form of passion. Trust me I know a bit about denial in that area."

"Well, you're incorrect in your assumption." Liam

glared. He didn't have any feelings for Gemma. She was a nuisance nothing more. "There aren't any tender feelings on either side. The girl irritates me to no end. I never did understand what Lily saw in her."

"That's too bad. I still have the betrothal contract I signed with Lady Gemma's father. We could have used it to our advantage."

Liam stared at his father with a blank expression. He'd actually signed the contract? How could he have done that? His father had reassured him he'd never force him to marry anyone.

"Excuse me could you repeat that? I don't think I heard you correctly." Liam hoped he'd heard wrong. Sadly he doubted he had. "You informed me the betrothal hadn't been finalized."

"That's correct," His father grinned. "However Devon hoped I'd change my mind and told me to keep the contract. All I have to do to make it legal is sign my name to it."

Liam blanched. His father was losing his mind. There wasn't a chance in hell he'd make him marry Lady Gemma. "But you're not going to, right

"So you are not willing to help?"

"I didn't say that." Liam shook his head. "I'm willing to hear the other plan you have. I'm hoping it is preferable to the latter."

"The other plan involves you basically kidnapping the girl and taking her to your sister in South Carolina."

Relief flooded him at his father's words. Calm now that the storm of anxiety fled his stomach, Liam took a deep breath and considered his father's other idea. He had to agree that the second plan held more appeal. It was preferable, but not that much better in the grand scheme of things. He would still be forced to spend a considerable amount of time in Lady Gemma's company. How would he be able to get through a voyage with her? They would have to take the Sea Rover for the crossing. No other ships were available, and their steamships were only in the planning stages of being built. If he had any luck, it wouldn't take more than three weeks to complete.

The bonus, of course, would be to see his sister and his new nephew. He sincerely wished to see them so that no price was too high for him to be able to spend time in their company. He would even be willing to get to know his brother-in-law as well. Maybe he would find a way to like the rat bastard. His father may have forgiven him for stealing Lily, but Liam didn't feel like he deserved such absolution. The man had a lot of audacity to run away with the daughter of Viscount Torrington—a former pirate. Liam would give him that much.

"That plan is more conceivable to accomplish," Liam said. "But is kidnapping really necessary? Do you believe Lady Gemma will be unwilling to go to live with Lily?"

"I honestly do not know," his father sighed. "I hate to tell you this, but I think you're going to need ammunition to get her out."

"Explain," Liam demanded.

"If you go in prepared Alfie won't have anything to argue about."

"How do you suggest I do that?"

His father grinned. It almost had a wicked tinge to it. "I'm going to sign this betrothal. Go to the bishop and demand a special license. With the right amount of money and the betrothal as evidence, he won't deny you."

"I fail to see why I need to go to such lengths."

"Alfie won't let Gemma go willingly. You're going to have to force his hand." His father paused and looked him in the eye. "I'm not telling you to marry the girl. Just use the tools I'm giving you to save her."

"All right I will go see the bishop now. Afterward, I will retrieve Gemma and bring her back here to plan our next move." Liam said.

"Good. I'd hate to disappoint your sister. I hope we are not too late to help Lady Gemma."

With those words, Liam got up and walked out of the study. He had never been a fan of Lady Gemma Kemsley, but he had never wished her ill will either. If she had more trouble than she could handle, Liam had no choice but to help her. His sister depended on him, and he had never let her down before—he certainly didn't plan on starting with Lady Gemma.

The chit had better be prepared to do everything necessary to leave her home. Liam didn't suffer fools and luckily for him he knew that she didn't either. No matter what he believed, her to be he had always been able to see the keen intelligence in her eyes. Perhaps with age she had also gained some maturity to go along with it.

ABOUT THE AUTHOR

USA TODAY Bestselling author, DAWN BROWER writes both historical and contemporary romance. There are always stories inside her head; she just never thought she could make them come to life. That creativity has finally found an outlet.

Growing up she was the only girl out of six children. She raised two boys into productive young men. There is never a dull moment in her life. Reading books is her favorite hobby and she loves all genres.

She is active on Facebook, Twitter, and Instagram. To follow her or can find more about her check out her website for the pertinent information:

www.authordawnbrower.com

bookbub.com/authors/dawn-brower

facebook.com/1DawnBrower

twitter.com/1DawnBrower

instagram.com/1DawnBrower

goodreads.com/dawnbrower

If It's Love (Amanda Mariel)

Odds of Love (Dawn Brower)

Believe In Love (Amanda Mariel)

Chance of Love (Dawn Brower)

Love and Holly (Amanda Mariel)

Love and Mistletoe (Dawn Brower

Bluestockings Defying Rogues

When An Earl Turns Wicked

A Lady Hoyden's Secret

One Wicked Kiss

Earl In Trouble

All the Ladies Love Coventry

One Less Scandalous Earl

Confessions of a Hellion

Coming Soon

The Vixen in Red

Marsden Descendants

Rebellious Angel

Tempting An American Princess

How to Kiss a Debutante

Loving an America Spy

Scheming with My Duke

Secluded with My Hellion

Coming Soon

Secrets of My Beloved

Spying on My Scoundrel

Shocked by My Vixen

Heart's Intent

One Heart to Give

Unveiled Hearts

Heart of the Moment

Kiss My Heart Goodbye

Heart in Waiting

Broken Curses

The Enchanted Princess

The Bespelled Knight

The Magical Hunt

Ever Beloved

Forever My Earl

Always My Viscount

Infinitely My Marquess

EternallyMyDuke

Kismet Bay

Once Upon a Christmas

New Year Revelation

All Things Valentine

Luck At First Sight

Endless Summer Days

A Witch's Charm

All Out of Gratitude

Christmas Ever After

AFTERWORD

Thank you so much for taking the time to read my book.

Your opinion matters!

Please take a moment to review this book on your favorite review site and share your opinion with fellow readers.

www.authordawnbrower.com

ACKNOWLEDGMENTS

Thanks Victoria Miller. You're the best.